BROKEN
ANGEL

A thrilling murder mystery, full of nail-biting suspense

DIANE M DICKSON

THE
BOOK
FOLKS

Paperback published by The Book Folks

London, 2018

ISBN 978-1-9832-8770-1

www.thebookfolks.com

For Ian.

Prologue

There had been rain in the night, not much but enough to drench the corpse, to turn what had been a pale, flimsy cotton nightdress, embroidered around the hem with forget-me-nots, into a grey shroud and to soak the long blond hair.

When the pathologist began his work, the body had already passed through the rigor stage and was decaying. There were flies, of course, and, given the location, there was already evidence that rats had taken a look – more than a look, truth be told.

The woman had been moved shortly after death, there was no discolouration of the body, no darkening of the tissue where it had lain.

There was no obvious trauma and it wasn't until later, in the cold atmosphere of the mortuary, that they found the marks of needles, the evidence of drug abuse that gave them the cause of death.

Another tale of despair ending in tragedy, but this time, not in a doorway, not in a stinking squat but here, in the peace of the woods, laid among the heather – left for nature.

It was obvious that the body had been posed and, in the end, the police concluded that some friend or lover, afraid of authority, had brought the woman here and left her with some degree of dignity, at least until the rats had begun their work.

If the reports were to be examined later, it would be true to say that the time spent trying to identify the woman, to find who had put her there, was probably not as vigorous as it could have been, but she was just one more druggie. She didn't show up on any missing person lists, she had nothing to identify her and even her teeth, neglected and rotten, weren't of any use in finding out who she had been. Her fingerprints and DNA were taken but they weren't on record. It was unusual though not unknown for there to be absolutely nothing, but they couldn't keep her forever and she was disposed of, buried rather than burned, just in case they needed to look again later. And although, of course, the case remained open, she was forgotten by almost everyone.

Tanya didn't forget her. It was the first corpse she had seen. There had been others since then, accident victims, some who died by their own hand, deliberately, and there were the murders, but they all had a name, a family, and someone to miss them. The woman in the woods did not. In her pale gown, her wet hair sticking to the once pretty face, she haunted.

Often in the quiet of the night, in her flat, Tanya would go over it all again, wonder what they had missed and where the people were who had the answers.

Chapter 1

It was always the same. They would make arrangements and Steve completely ignored them. It wasn't a lapse of memory, most of the time he just didn't listen, or couldn't be bothered to stick to what they'd agreed. Sarah paced back and forth in the smelly, steamy, damp mall of the service area. It was warm and muggy, filled with the stink of greasy burgers, whining kids, grumpy fat women and lecherous teens who, for some unfathomable reason, thought she gave a damn about their opinion of her. The rage grew, she still couldn't see him anywhere.

Finally, she'd had enough. They had said ten minutes by the Costa outlet and it had been – what – bloody twenty already. She had come straight here, well almost. A quick stop to pick up a couple of sandwiches and drinks but for heaven's sake, how long could it take to have a pee?

Maybe he was already back at the car. Yeah, that would be typical. They would agree where to meet and then he'd wander off and do his own thing. He was probably sitting in the bloody front seat right now, texting and playing with his phone in comfort.

Furious didn't begin to cover it.

Sarah stepped out into the miserable drizzle and, head down, arms clutched in front of her juggling the picnic and her bag, she scuttled towards the Mondeo.

Great, bloody great, there was still no sign of him.

The car park was jammed. Well of course it was, Thursday evening at the end of the school holidays. One last chance before the start of term. Everybody and their bloody kids off for the weekend, though if this weather lasted it'd be another typical English wash out. The wind whipped at her coat and blew the drizzle into her face. "Shit, shit, shit. Steve sodding Blakely," she muttered under her breath, "I'm done with you, I really am." When they had talked about this break, she had wanted Benidorm, Majorca, anywhere but here, anywhere but the English Lakes where it always rains, absolutely every time. She kicked the car tyres in frustration.

She wouldn't go back into the services, would not go and search for him. There was a spare key in a little plastic box hidden under the wheel arch, stuck with a magnet, apparently. Okay, he told her it was for emergencies only, but as far as Sarah was concerned this was an emergency. She knew it wouldn't start the car, but it would at least get her inside and out of the weather.

The strap of her bag was slung over her shoulder, no way did she want it going on the filthy wet floor. She hoisted it up, settled it more securely. She wouldn't have brought it if she'd known it was going to be this wet, but she loved it. Yes, she'd spent more than she should, yes, Steve had a paddy, but sod him. It was her money and she had always paid her share of the rent and the running costs on the flat.

She crouched by the rear wheel, hands on the cold wet metal, it was a struggle to balance on her haunches. The dirty puddles made kneeling an impossibility. It was filthy in the space where the key should be. When he'd told her where he was going to put it she'd questioned the sense of it. "Won't it just fall off when we go over bumps?" He'd given her one of those looks. Well he'd been wrong; the sodding thing had gone. Just as she was about to give up, her fingertips touched it.

"Can I help you?"

From her position down beside the tyre, all that was visible was a pair of wet, grey trainers and rain-speckled jeans. "Bloody hell, Steve, where have you been?"

"Is this your car?"

She turned, squinted, and peered up into the drizzle. Ah, it wasn't Steve. She took in a breath to tell this person to mind his own business, but then she saw the wallet. He was leaning towards her. In his hand was a small, dark coloured folder, on one side a picture. There was no way for her to know whether it was the owner of the voice, she hadn't seen him properly yet. On the other side was the badge, a gold metal shield. She had never seen one before but knew what it must be.

"Ah. Right. No, it's not actually my car but it is my boyfriend's, I'm Sarah, Sarah Dickinson, he's Steve."

As she scuttled back, her shoes scraped on the gravel, it was awkward and clumsy. She reached upwards, holding the door handle for support as she uncurled. She pulled her hair away from her face, tucked it behind her ears. The man was taller than she, and much older, but broad, a bit rough looking. He was wearing a black leather jacket, the soggy-looking jeans, and no hat, so his short dark hair dripped onto his face. His head was tipped to one side, eyebrows raised.

Sarah peered towards the service area. Where was Steve?

"So, it's not your car?"

"No, as I say it's my partner's and he's in there." She pointed at the building across the expanse of parking. We were supposed to meet up, but I decided to come back to the car and there's a spare key, under here." She waved a hand towards the rear bumper.

"Wouldn't it be easier just to wait for him?"

"I've done that. I've waited ages for him and I don't know where he is. It's okay. He's always doing this, and I just decided I'd wait in the car."

"Have you tried ringing him?"

She sighed. "Yes. I've rung him, of course I've rung him, but his sodding phone's turned off or something. Look, he went to the toilet, I went to the ladies, and we agreed to meet by the Costa place. He's not come back yet. He's probably in the games area, or maybe in one of the shops but honestly, he's always doing this and it's not a problem, really."

The man just stood and looked at her, the rain was heavier and, struggling with embarrassment and frustration, she wished he would go away.

"So, what are you going to do?"

"Oh look. I'll just go back inside, see if I can find him." She reached to gather her belongings, but the black clad arm stretched past to collect the shopping in the sopping carrier bag from the roof.

"Tell you what. Why don't you come and sit in my car? I'll call inside, and we'll get an announcement on the loud-speaker."

"Oh, well, yeah that's nice of you but really, you know, there's no need." Before she had finished speaking, the stranger stepped away, pulled out his mobile, bowed his head to keep the rain out of his eyes as he muttered into the handset.

"Right that's sorted. Come on, my car's just over here." He turned, still carrying the sandwiches and strode off. There was no other choice but to follow and, after all, it would get her out of the wet. Steve was going to be so embarrassed, hearing his name on the loudspeaker, having to explain to the police what he'd been doing. She couldn't resist the grin that spread across her face as she quickened her pace to keep up.

The car wasn't one of the blue and whites, it was a van, dark coloured, parked around the side, near the motel.

6

What could they be doing, hidden here? Maybe it was about terrorism, or maybe drugs. She felt a frisson of fear mixed with excitement. She looked more closely at the policeman. He was a bit scruffy, unkempt really. Undercover, he must be. It was a dangerous job, you had to admire that. She couldn't wait to tell Steve. Thinking of her boyfriend irritated her all over again.

"You'd better get inside." He slid open the side door with a rattle and Sarah clambered in. There were bottles of water in a torn plastic wrapper, he pulled two of them out, held one out to her and then opened the other, gulping back a half of it. His hands were not quite steady. "Is it dangerous? What you're doing."

He shrugged his shoulders, of course he couldn't tell her. She pulled open the bottle top and raised it to her lips.

Chapter 2

Charlie Lambert pushed the heavy wooden door open with his elbow. The uniformed officer behind the desk grinned across at him. "Morning Detective Inspector." He smiled back, shook his head, a bit embarrassed. It was still new enough to be a thrill. Acknowledging the couple of people waiting on the benches, he strode on past to the 'staff only' doors and up to the office.

There were only two people in the squad room, both constables, both working on computers. Kate Lewis and Sue Rollinson. He waved across at them as they looked up and then he carried on through. His office was tucked into the far end; *his* office, it still made him smile. It had been two weeks since his promotion was finalised and one since he had taken over this small space. He pulled the chair away from his desk with his foot and dropped various bits and pieces on the desk and the floor. As the computer booted, he took the cover from the tall cup of latte and sipped as he scrolled through the overnight reports. He starred a couple of things to go back to: a robbery at an off licence, and a mugging in the town centre.

He swivelled his chair around so that he could see out of the window, see the roofs and roads, and the endless lines of cars snaking through the rush hour. Five minutes and then he'd collect one of the constables from the office and get on with it. He could walk to the off licence and the victim of the mugging wouldn't leave hospital until later in the day, so he could put that off until she was home.

When the phone rang he had a mouth full of pastry and should have left it until he was able to speak but the red light on the base was flashing. The Chief Inspector's office. There was no option but to mumble through the mouth full of food at Glynis, Bob Scunthorpe's secretary. "Hold on a sec."

She chuckled at the other end of the line.

"He wants to see you, soon as you can manage it."

"Okay, five minutes."

"Sorry to interrupt your breakfast, Charlie." With another giggle she was gone.

He took the time for a quick stop at the toilets on the way to the third floor. It wouldn't look good to arrive with crumbs on his shirt and grease on his chin.

DCI Bob Scunthorpe looked up at the knock on his door and waved a hand, beckoning Charlie inside. "I won't keep you long, Inspector."

This was never going to be a lengthy interview, there was no invitation to sit, just a report held out for him to read.

"As you see we've got a woman missing. She hasn't been gone long and normally we would be waiting to see how things pan out. Very likely it's just the result of some sort of row and she's taken herself off to make the boyfriend worry. The problem is him, the boyfriend, partner, whatever. Have a look at the attached printouts."

Charlie flipped the papers over, read the copy of Tweets and Facebook posts. He screwed up his nose. "Hmm, nasty sir. He's not pulling his punches, and these are getting lots of reposts."

"Yes, quite. Get over there will you, see if you can calm things down. Take somebody with you, make it look as though we're giving it all our attention."

"Yes, thank you, sir." Back in the squad room there was only one constable still working: Sue, more properly Suhrita but anglicised, probably for convenience more than anything. Newly promoted to CID, there hadn't been much time to get to know her, but when Charlie told her to grab her coat and follow him down to the car park she beamed at him.

Once in his car he handed over the sheaf of papers, then gave her a quick precis of the situation.

"We've got to go and see a Steve Blakely. Created a bit of a fuss yesterday at the motorway services."

"Shouldn't that just be dealt with by the motorway patrol, sir?"

"Yes, normally, and they were on the scene at first. Anyway, he reckons his girlfriend went missing while he was in the toilets."

"Right?"

"Well, they got separated and when he couldn't find her he asked them to make an announcement – they did that, but nothing, and he became a bit agitated."

"How old are we talking, is this a teenager?"

"No, a woman, it's down there." He wagged a hand towards the papers, sounding a bit impatient. She blushed.

"Anyway, when she didn't turn up – after the announcement and so on, going everywhere looking for her, pestering women to check the ladies, all that stuff – he was pretty upset and then to cap it all they tried to charge him for parking because he'd been there for more than two hours."

Sue gave a short laugh, "Bloody typical."

Charlie grinned back at her, his brown eyes sparkling. "Yeah I know."

"So, what is it that we're doing now then?"

"Turns out he's a well-known blogger. Gets back home, starts bleating on, blogging, Facebooking, Tweeting – all about how the police didn't take him seriously; his girl is missing and all anyone cares about is the parking money."

Sue drew in a hiss of breath. "Nasty. So, the local bods, what do they think?"

"Not really sure, no sign of anything in or around the car. She's not answering her phone."

Sue shook her head, "Well duh, of course she's not. If they had a row."

"He insists they didn't. Anyway, the Chief Inspector wants us to go and have a word. Try and calm things down, try and stop the Twitter storm."

"Bit late for that. It's bloody mayhem. Have you looked at these print outs?"

"Yeah, well we'll have to do what we can."

* * *

Steven Blakely was obviously distressed. They held up their warrant cards and watched the colour drain from his face. "Christ, what is it? Have you found her? Oh shit."

Charlie held up a hand, "No, no sorry. Mr Blakely, please calm down. We don't have any news, we just need to talk to you."

The other man squeezed his eyes shut, blew out a breath. "I thought, well for a minute I thought, you know – plain clothes and all that. Come in." He stood back to let them pass.

"I'm sorry, Mr Blakely, we didn't mean to upset you. We've been asked to come around and have a chat about what happened yesterday, at the services."

"So, are you looking for her? What have you done to find her?"

This was delicate, if they told him they'd done nothing it was hardly going to encourage him to cut back on the online furore. Sue lowered herself to the leather sofa, fished in her bag for her notebook. Charlie introduced himself.

He leaned forward, looked the other man in the eye, "We need more information. We need to get things organised. We have the report from the officers you spoke to yesterday, it's been passed to us and…"

"You haven't done anything, have you? Sarah is missing, and you haven't done anything." They watched his face flush with anger, saw the fists clench.

"We're putting together the information. Thing is, Mr Blakely, Sarah is an adult, she hasn't yet been missing for twenty-four hours. There was no sign of any struggle, no call for help, nothing to alert us to foul play. Look, let's get some more details down and then we'll decide the best way forward. Do you have a picture of Sarah? A recent one."

In answer he held out his phone, the image of a young woman, long blonde hair, a big grin, looked back at them. Steve turned the phone back towards himself, stared down at the screen. "That was just before we set off. She had that new top on, wanted a picture for Facebook." His eyes flooded.

Charlie spoke quietly, "I'll give you our contact details and if you could email us that picture it'll help. Mr Blakely, could we ask you to keep this off the internet for the moment? I understand that it's the default response these days, but it could hamper any enquiries we might have to make."

He didn't answer, just gave a short nod, "So you will be making some then; enquiries?"

"We'll certainly look into it, yes. See if there is any more that we need to be doing, monitor the situation closely." He wasn't happy, but they'd done what they could for the moment.

Chapter 3

As Charlie drove away, Sue began to make notes.

"I don't know how you can do that. I read or write in the car and I'm puking after the first corner."

"It's never bothered me actually, we made loads of car trips when I was a kid, they were boring, you know, two brothers being a nuisance. I guess I just got used to it."

"Anyway, what d'you reckon about Blakely? He's pretty hyper, isn't he?"

She closed the notebook, "Yes, more than you would have expected, to be honest. It must have been quite a row, if that's what this is about. I know he said they didn't have one, I don't know whether to believe that or not, but it's a bit odd. You would think that if they'd had a bit of a barny, she'd have turned up by now or got in touch anyway – makes you wonder. Maybe they did, and it got very heated, more than he's letting on. He said they'd been together three years, yeah? It was a nice flat, looked like a nice home, it's quite a reaction to just bugger off. He seemed a pretty decent sort. But you can never tell, can you?"

Charlie chewed his lip, thought for a while, "Why don't we head down to the services and have a word with the manager? Let's just make sure there's nothing up, nothing we're missing. You're probably going to be right, it was a row, but let's see. There's going to be CCTV to look at. Tell me again, what did the first responders say about that?"

"Hmm" – she read from her phone. "From this report they had a quick look. She left the building with some shopping and then disappeared into the crowd, couldn't see the car that well, the place was humming, last weekend of the summer you know, and actually, I think they were more involved with calming things down. He was pretty fired up and then trying to make him pay for the car park didn't help..."

"So, he's got a bit of a temper, then?"

"I'd say so, he had to struggle a bit while we were there, at first, did you notice? Could he really have done something to her? Nah, surely if it was that, he'd just have driven off?"

Charlie nodded, "Yes, that'd be logical, but then, people don't always do what's logical. We'll get them to track her phone if that's not already been done. We'll get the recording in from the cameras and then at least we can show we've done what we could. She'll probably get in touch with him when she's calmed down anyway. Can you get that in motion when we get back? I have to pop out for an hour. Got to go home."

"Problem?"

"No, Joshua's having his inoculations and I told Carol I'd go with her."

"Aw, yeah I'd forgotten you've got a baby. How is he?"

Charlie laughed, "He's fine thanks, but Carol's not too good right now." He paused but it was good to unload a bit, "She's suffering with post-natal depression, Doctor's got her on some new medicine. It's a sod you know, because we wanted a baby, tried for a while before she got

14

pregnant, then she was so thrilled when he was born – it doesn't make sense to me that she could be depressed."

Sue leaned forward, touched Charlie on the arm. "Post-natal depression, it's nothing to do with whether or not you wanted the baby. It's more complicated. My sister-in-law had it, it's a bitch but she got better, had another sprog with no problems. At least your Carol, she's getting looked after eh?"

"Yeah." He dredged up a smile and glanced across at her. "I'll have to show you some pictures. I don't like to do it too much at work. Don't want to be a baby bore and all that but, Joshua, well he's different, he's brilliant."

"Yeah, course he is. I'd love to see them, really." She pointed out of the window, "It's this exit. Don't worry, I can get things started back at work while you're gone."

* * *

The manager of the service area was on his way to middle-aged, sweaty in his shiny suit. His office was little more than a cubicle in the upstairs space, there were boxes of supplies in the corner, charts on the wall showing staff schedules.

He sat behind the chipped desk, folded his hands in front of him. "He was very threatening, that's why I called for help. I mean, my staff were just doing their jobs, there was no need for him to be so belligerent. I had a late start, my deputy did what he thought was correct, stuck to the rules as laid down. It was all kicking off when I came in. I don't know why he has you people involved now, if he can't look after his girlfriend then it's his business."

Sue flipped open her notebook, spoke to him quietly, non-committal, "We've spoken to Mr Blakely this morning, he is still very upset about what happened."

"She hasn't turned up then?"

"No, I'm afraid not. We've seen the original reports, is there anything else you can tell us? We know Ms Dickinson used the facilities, did some shopping, and then went out to the car park. Now, from what we hear it's not possible to see what happened after that."

"No, well it was mayhem here yesterday afternoon. Parking was full, people dashing in and out. Some of the cameras went down as well. Not sure what happened, they came back on again later and the technicians couldn't find a reason. Typical." He tutted. "Technology never works when you need it to. Anyway, from what my staff told me, told the police, she went into the M&S – that's on the camera – bought some stuff, paid with a card and really that's about all we know."

"When you say she bought stuff, do you know just what exactly?" Sue asked.

He raised his eyes, dabbed at his sweating forehead with a piece of tissue. "Not really, you'd need to speak directly to them, if it's important."

"Ah right, we'll do that then. It might give us an idea as to her thinking. Did she buy enough for two? Something just for herself? Maybe something to take with them to their holiday place?"

The manager nodded, "Oh right. I see. Well, I'll ring down, tell them you need a word."

Charlie glanced at his watch, pushed back from the desk. "That's very helpful, thank you. We need to speak to your deputy as well."

"He won't be in now until, erm…" He consulted a desk pad. "Tuesday, yes. So, she probably just went off, either hitched or maybe even met somebody else, by arrangement, or just in a temper."

"Bit unusual for a young woman to hitchhike these days, isn't it?" Charlie asked.

"Oh, you'd be surprised. Lorry drivers, they pick people up, it's company isn't it and well, you know."

Sue raised her eyebrows, "No, we don't know. What is it you're implying?"

He blushed, dabbed at his head again with the tissue. "Oh, nothing, nothing. Just sometimes, women, well people, they do odd things. Anyway, if that's all, I've got to get on." He waved a hand over his cluttered desk, evidence of his busy day.

"That'd be great." Charlie held out a card with his contact details on. "Thanks for your help."

As they stood to leave, George Simpson waved a hand towards the window, "Working here you know, you'd be surprised what goes on. People rowing, storming out on each other, blagging lifts, ringing taxis. There's no need to think anyone else was involved, just her, her on her own." He bent to pick up his phone as Sue and Charlie let themselves out and back down to the main concourse.

"You know that's a point, isn't it?" Sue was buckling herself in, tearing open the bar of chocolate she'd picked up when they spoke to the staff in the M&S on the way through the mall. "She could have rung a taxi, if they'd had a row. That's something else we should look at. I'll see if some of the civilian bods at the office can get onto that when we get back."

"So, you think that she took herself off voluntarily, do you? Would you really do that, on your own, even if you were furious with him, your partner?" Charlie pulled the car into the endless line of traffic, slipped between the vehicles in the middle lane, out into the third and then put his foot down, glancing at his watch again.

"I don't see what else it can be, do you? I mean the place was crowded, you can't kidnap someone from the middle of a crowded car park without anyone noticing. No, she's buggered off, either on her own or with her fancy man, I'd put money on it. Bit mean though, not letting him know. Course, I reckon that manager could be right. Maybe she went on her own, just got fed up and left. Grabbed a cab."

"But where would she go? Wouldn't she go back to their house? Also, there is all her stuff. According to Charlie it's still in the boot of the car, surely if she was leaving him she'd take at least her overnight gear with her.

It's odd, and the more you think about it, the odder it seems."

Chapter 4

The worst thing was not being able to remember. When Sarah first woke in the dingy little room, she thought that they were in the Lakes. That was where they had been going, she knew that. She looked around her, the bed was narrow, the curtains thin, limp and dirty looking. She was under the covers fully dressed. Why was she in bed with her clothes on? Where were her things? Where was Steve?

She called his name. If this was the cosy hotel he had promised her then she wasn't impressed. She wasn't staying here. It was foul, it smelled bad.

This couldn't be it, something had gone wrong. She shook her head, trying to clear her mind. She could remember packing the car, they'd been laughing, he promised her that if it rained he'd take her to Spain for certain. She remembered locking the flat, he'd been driving, and then after that everything became confused. She thought she had bought them a picnic, she didn't remember eating it.

She pushed up from the bed and staggered to the window, pulled back the curtains, but couldn't see outside. There were shutters nailed across the inside of the frame. That wasn't right. Her heart began to race, she called

Steve's name again. She ran to the door, but when she twisted and rattled at the knob it wouldn't open.

She pounded on the wood. This wasn't a B&B in the Lakes, this was a nightmare. She screamed.

Round and round the room, opening the wardrobe full of old clothes, banging on the door, screaming, none of it did any good, and still she couldn't remember anything about arriving here, about coming to bed.

She wanted Steve, he was a pain in the bum sometimes, but right now she wanted his arms, she wanted him to fix this for her.

There was the sound of a car. She was sure it was a car, then the slam of a door. She pounded again, screamed to be let out.

For a long time, nothing happened. She still couldn't remember, not being able to remember was the worst.

Eventually, she heard footsteps on the stairs, the rattle of a key. The knob turned.

She was afraid; she was very, very afraid. She ran back to the horrible bed and pulled the thin blanket over her, huddled in the corner with her arms wrapped around her and her knees drawn up. Tears came, she couldn't stop them.

As the door opened she whispered into the nasty dark room. "Steve. Is that you, Steve?"

Chapter 5

Nothing came up overnight, no sign of the missing woman.

Charlie left Carol and the baby sleeping after a difficult night. Calling in for breakfast, he went the bacon sandwich route. He reckoned walking the floor for hours had earned him some comfort food. He powered up the computer, scanned the night reports and turned the fans on to rid the air of the smell of grease and coffee.

He called Sue into his office, "Got an email from the M&S outlet at the services. Seems that girl bought a sort of picnic: drinks, sandwiches, crisps."

"For one or two?"

He glanced at the email, "Enough for two, two different drinks, two different sarnies."

"Hmm, so either she was planning to meet someone, or she had no intention of going off on her own, leaving her partner. I can't say I accept that she was meeting someone else. Why would you do it like that, make it so complicated? If she wanted out, she could have just gone, any time. From home, you know, more organised."

"I suppose. I have to say it does seem as though they were just on their way together and something unexpected happened. Did you get anything back about the phone?" Charlie asked.

"Yes, there's a report. You should have a copy. It's dead apparently. The last signal was from the services and then nothing." They stared at each other across the little office. Charlie nodded and pushed up from his chair. "I'm going to have a word with the Chief Inspector, there's something up here. I'm thinking we need to move this up a notch, what do you reckon? It's more than twenty-four hours and there's been nothing."

Sue tucked her long hair behind her ears, frowned and then gave a nod. "Yes. Back to speak to the boyfriend again, is it?"

Charlie grunted, grabbed his coat. "I'll see you in the car park. We'll take my car."

"Great, mine's an old banger. I don't think it'd give the right impression."

Charlie grinned, "Fair enough."

* * *

After a short interview with the Chief Inspector, Charlie walked across the car park. He could see Sue, pacing back and forth, her phone in front of her, he grinned. He wondered if she believed all that stuff about brain tumours, or maybe she simply preferred to use the hands-free and ear buds. He waved for her to get into the passenger seat as he plipped the key. As they pulled out into the main road, Sue asked him about his wife and the baby.

"Yeah, Joshua was a bit fractious last night, kept us up, but apparently as soon as I left he went to sleep and he's been soundo ever since. Little sod."

"Carol okay?"

He nodded, and they left it.

* * *

When Steve Blakely opened the door, they were shocked at the dishevelled state of him. His eyes were dark ringed and bloodshot, his clothes wrinkled, and they caught the faint, unwashed smell of body odour. "Have you heard anything? Have you found anything out?"

Charlie raised a hand, indicated the door to the living room, and he stood aside to let them walk through.

"I'm sorry, Mr Blakely, we have no real news. We have made more enquiries and, in light of what we've learned I'm here to tell you that we are going to widen the investigation. I do need to ask you some more questions. Look, you don't seem well. Can we make you a cup of tea? Have you eaten anything?"

"No, no. I've been up all night. I can't eat. I can't rest. I just keep wondering where she is. I've been dialling her number over and over, but it just goes to voice mail. See I thought she'd be here, I thought maybe she'd got in a huff and made her own way back. We love each other, we really do. Okay we have rows now and then, she gets impatient with me, but I'm sick of this. I just want her back."

Sue went into the hallway, found the kitchen and filled the kettle. She took bread from the wooden box on the counter, stuck a couple of pieces in the toaster and threw tea bags into three mugs.

In the meantime, Charlie explained that Sarah's phone was untraceable after the services, that even if it was turned off they would have been able to find it, so that was cause for concern. He told him about the picnic and watched helplessly as Steve sank further into his misery, saw fear crawl into his eyes. She had bought their favourite sandwiches.

"So, you hadn't actually had a row then? Only, you just said, maybe she was in a huff, perhaps she had left because she was angry."

Steve shook his head, "No, no we hadn't had a row but, well I'd kept her waiting and she hated that. That's why I took a while to say anything, I thought she was just sulking somewhere and she'd turn up once she'd made her point."

There was a tingle of foreboding in Charlie's gut, but he nodded and smiled.

They tried to persuade him to have a friend come and stay but he wouldn't agree, insisting that he wanted to be on his own. Sue had brought the tea and toast through and, though he managed a half slice, all he wanted was the drink.

"We'll be in touch, Steve, we'll keep you informed. Try not to worry too much. There could still be a simple explanation. It could be that she just needed some time, you know?"

They could tell by his expression that he didn't believe them but there was no more comfort they could offer.

Chapter 6

"Okay, we've got an incident room. They're setting that up right now. I've had them generate the operational name. Kate's going to be assigned and a couple of extra bods, not enough, but a team at least. Paul Harris, Dan Price. I haven't worked with them, have you?" Charlie asked.

Sue was gathering the reports together, she shook her head. "I know Kate quite well, but no, not the others. It's a bit of a bind isn't it, it takes longer to work together when it's a new team. Can't be helped I suppose, sickness, leave and stuff. It'll be okay though."

Charlie shrugged and pulled a face. "Posters will be ready in the next couple of hours. We'll put them at the service areas where she went missing and the ones before and after. We're trying for a press conference, but we need to get Steven Blakely on board for that, always better with a partner. What have I forgotten?"

Sue shook her head. She knew how important this was to him, "It's moving on, you've got it sorted. Are they doing a search around the place she disappeared?"

"Yes, some uniforms are out now, not as many as we'd like but we have to manage. They're around the services, up and down the motorway on the northbound side. Not much point spreading them too thinly, looking at the other side at the moment, although I suppose if she was in a car it's not that far to the exit and then back on again. We haven't initiated a full-on missing person search yet, dogs and what have you, but maybe that's next. What do you reckon, Sue? Did they have a row, does Blakely know where she is?"

She puffed out her cheeks. "Dunno. There's still a chance that she just went off with someone else, but I have to say it seems unlikely, and the phone thing is a worry. I suppose she could know about tracing, but most people don't. She's a bookshop manager, would she know about that stuff? I suppose if she read a lot, but no, not that feasible. If she really wanted to vanish she might have destroyed it, but for most people letting go of their phones is pretty last ditch, isn't it?"

Sometimes you just know. When the phone rings it sounds as it always does but you just know.

As the mobile in Charlie's pocket chimed they looked at each other and Charlie sighed; rubbed his hands over his face.

Because sometimes, you just know.

He took the call, it wasn't long, and was answered in monosyllables. "They found a phone. It's in bits. Come on we'll go down there."

* * *

The rain of the day before had abated but puddles and mud were everywhere. A uniformed constable pointed to the trees. "It's just over there. Could be any old phone of course but there we are. We've marked it."

Peering down at the little pile of broken plastic beside the marker, it was true, it could be any old phone. But the shiny pink cover, that was girly. Charlie leaned in and took a few pictures with his own phone, zooming in on the case.

Coming away they spoke to the uniform sergeant, he had already arranged for the bits to be photographed and collected, marked as evidence, once Charlie had seen them in situ. He had a team looking further afield, just in case there was anything more. They thanked him, ducked back under the tape and went into the services. It seemed there were uniforms everywhere, talking to the public, sticking up the missing person posters. It made it all very real.

The manager met them, fussing, and worrying. "How long before we can get back to normal? This is having a direct effect on sales. People glance in, see all the uniforms, they think there's been a terrorist incident or something. A quick visit to the loos and then they're off again. I don't know what you're looking for. What are you looking for? She's not here, is she? I don't see why we have all this upheaval."

"Well, Mr Simpson, I can't give you an answer, I'm afraid. We need to find out what, if anything, happened to this young woman. You do see that, don't you?"

"Yes, yes of course I do but couldn't you just be – oh I don't know – a bit more discrete, quicker?"

Charlie sighed. "Not really, in these early days the most important thing is to try and find people who might have seen her. People who come through here regularly. Naturally, with it being the start of the weekend there would have been a different mix, day trippers instead of business men, anyone passing on holiday, or off for a short break. We'll need to try and catch them coming back. On the other side for that, of course, but for now at least I'm afraid there's nothing I can do about it. We'll try not to inconvenience you more than necessary."

George Simpson didn't answer, gave a huff and spun away, taking a couple of steps in the direction of his office.

Charlie raised his voice. "I'll need to know about the staff."

He spun around again. "How do you mean?"

"I'll need access to personnel files, find out who is who really, anything unusual. We will need to have a look at the people who are here regularly."

"Well I don't know if that's possible. I mean, surely that's an intrusion, what about their rights, their civil liberty, all that stuff?"

"I'm afraid that comes second when we're investigating a crime. If you can't help we'll contact your HR department directly. Leave that with us."

With another huff of impatience and a glare which took in the whole area the manager stomped away from them.

"Probably a waste of time, Sue, but run a check on him. See if we've had dealings. We'll get off, go and see Steven Blakely, show him the picture of the phone case, what's left of it. He'll probably freak out but it's the quickest way to find out whether or not we're wasting our time with it."

"Mine's like that. They're dead common."

"I know. Of course, I know, but if it's definitely not hers the quicker we know the better."

* * *

They could tell immediately that he recognised it. He reached out and pulled Charlie's phone closer, peered at the small image. "God. Where was this?"

"It was near the services; do you think it could be hers? Bear in mind that they are pretty common."

"Yeah, yeah, right." He grasped at the straw. "Yes, of course that's right. But she had one like this: pink, sparkly. That little sticker, the kitten, she had one like that."

"And what make is her phone?" Sue asked quietly.

"Galaxy. Samsung."

Charlie nodded and took his own phone from Steve's shaking hand. There was no need to confirm that it was the make and model of the one they had found. The name was there, obvious on the image.

"I'm going to have a family liaison officer come and stay with you, Steve. If you hear anything from Sarah, or think of anything, she'll be able to get in touch with us quickly, or I could arrange for a man if you'd prefer."

He nodded, buried his face in his hand. "Whatever, I don't mind." As they let themselves out of the front door, they could hear the muffled sound of his sobs.

Chapter 7

They buckled themselves into Charlie's car. "Right," he said, "back to the office I reckon. I need to speak to Bob Scunthorpe. It's vital now that we put an appeal on the telly before the end of the day."

The incident room had been sorted, computers moved in and a picture of Sarah pinned to the board against the wall, a timeline underneath it.

Charlie walked to the notice board, waited and looked around. The two new men and Kate Lewis stood when he arrived; they formed a vague semi-circle between the desks. Sue joined them, and grinned. She didn't want to appear standoffish, but she had enjoyed working closely with the boss and it was going to be hard now being part of a bigger team.

"Okay, Operation Archer." They nodded in acknowledgement. It made it real, gave it a hook.

"Any of you worked together before? Paul, Dan, do you know Kate and Sue?"

The taller of the two men nodded, "Me and Dan have but not with the girls." Kate glared at him, her mouth a tight line. He didn't seem to notice.

"Well, I guess we all need to get to know each other." Charlie had picked up on the spark of disapproval, he'd have to watch that, nip any sort of antagonism in the bud. He was surprised, mostly because it was done with no real ill will, giving the impression of ignorance rather than insult. He'd maybe have a word with Paul at some stage, not yet though. Not until they had a chance to meld a bit. "Carry on getting yourselves sorted and then we can go over the background and what have you." He waved to the two civilian tech guys who had been sorting out cables, screens and computers in the small room. "Thanks." They left with a thumbs-up and a smile.

They took a few minutes to lay claim to work spaces, adjust their chairs, and to settle into the idea. Charlie moved in front of the board. "Right, if I can have your attention for a minute. You've all read the background to this." He glanced around the small group of nodding heads. "We've got help from the guys who cover the motorway, when they can fit it in between chasing nutters who are speeding and so on. The traffic officers have been briefed but of course, they're limited in what they can do. But the more eyes out there the better chance we have of finding her. I think, for the moment the services would be the best use of our time. We have so little information and, typically, the CCTV isn't the help it should be. Sarah Dickinson isn't very easy to spot once she gets between the parked cars. There are people everywhere, the visibility was a bit naff, with the rain and all, so – our best hope is that somebody saw her. You know what to do people. Let's find a witness, yeah?" He pointed to the two women sitting towards the back of the room, "Kate, can you stay here? Man the phones and what have you."

The first hours were important, before time blurred memories and the world moved on, they had so very little to work with and they'd lost more than a day already. Charlie went through the notes again, looking for something that might give him an idea. There was nothing. The woman had vanished without fuss, without notice.

* * *

Charlie brought up the area on Google earth. They had found the phone just beyond the parking area, opposite the hotel and near to the wooded land. Had it been tossed there from the car park? The troops on the ground would be looking for footprints and tracks, of course. But it was so very wet, and the area was used by dog walkers, churning up the ground while their animals dug and snuffled and crapped. They more than likely wouldn't have noticed the phone, not with the rain in their faces. It was smashed, so of no interest. Sarah could have walked or been taken through the trees, she could have been forced into a car at this quieter area of the services, or maybe neither of those theories was true and this wasn't even her phone after all. They had the SIM but unearthing the secrets was down to the technical nerds and it was in a long queue for attention down in the IT department. He'd see if any of the new team had contacts down there, maybe they could speed things up.

There were a few groups of houses and they would widen the search to include them, but this was the motorway, the main route from London to Birmingham. What were the chances that she was anywhere in the area by now? Pretty remote in reality. There was no use hiding from it: unless they had a huge stroke of luck, finding her – if she didn't want to be found – was nigh on impossible taking into account what they had to work with.

Sue had stopped on the way out and peered over his shoulder. "Any ideas?"

He rubbed his hands over his face, "All we can do at this point is stick to protocol, follow the usual routines and hope for a great dollop of luck. I'm meeting with the Chief Inspector in a few minutes, I've got nothing to tell him and no brilliant ideas."

Sue touched his arm, "He'll understand, he's been here, done this. Don't try and flannel him, just stick to the facts."

"Yeah, thanks Mum."

She laughed and turned away, disappearing into the corridor to catch up with the two men.

He rang home, spoke briefly to Carol and told her he might be late. She seemed well, unless she was burying her feelings – supporting him, just as she always did. He picked up his notes and went through the squad room, speaking over his shoulder as he went. "Kate, give the FLO a ring, tell her to get Blakely geared up for the online appeal, the sooner the better. Once I have the go ahead from Bob Scunthorpe we should be able to get something out this evening."

"Right, oh, before you go, that manager... the bloke at the services. George..." Kate ran a finger down one of the papers on her desk, "Simpson, yeah. We did get a couple of minor hits. Eight years ago, he was questioned about an incident of indecent exposure. A couple of young girls in a park said he'd wagged his dick at them. He said he had been caught short and had been peeing in the bushes. He was cautioned. Then six months after that he was picked up in a sweep of kerb crawlers. He insisted that he was there innocently, his car was playing up and he'd had to pull over to give it time to cool down. Again, it was a case of maybe yes, maybe no, so they gave him the benefit of the doubt."

Charlie screwed up his face, "Hmm, insignificant little man. A bit unsavoury but... I can't see him grabbing a woman. Not in his own back yard."

"No, but he would know his way around the area I suppose, and he was on the spot. Might be worthwhile having a look. Give you something to tell the Chief at least."

"Maybe. Maybe. Anyway, I reckon once the appeal's over we'll help with manning phones for a bit, something might pop. Fingers crossed."

The phone on the desk rang.

He glanced over at Kate in the corner, who was watching him as he lifted the receiver.

He replaced the phone, punched the air, "Yes. Dan's got someone who thinks they saw her. A woman, they're bringing her in. Movement, not much but something. Hope for the best, Kate."

Chapter 8

She was a small woman, middle aged, dressed in trousers and a padded jacket. Though she tried, she was unable to keep the air of excitement out of her eyes and her voice as she answered their questions. She accepted a cup of tea, piled her bag and coat on the chair beside where she sat, peering around at the lounge they had brought her to.

"Thank you so much for your time, Mrs Brett." Charlie smiled across the little coffee table.

"Are you going to record it?"

"No, not at all. We just need you to tell us again what you said to the officer at the services. You saw this young woman?" Charlie held out a copy of the picture they had on the posters.

"Yes, on Thursday. My mother's in hospital you see. I have to go and see her every day. On the way home I stop for a cup of coffee. It's stressful, the hospital."

"I'm sorry. I hope it's nothing too serious."

"Oh, I don't think she'll be coming home again but..." There was a small shrug of the narrow shoulders. "What can you do?"

There was no answer. As the moment of silence grew Kate leaned forward, prompted gently. "So, you saw this person?"

"Yes, that's right. I wouldn't have noticed her I don't suppose but for the bag."

"Bag?"

"Yes, she had one of those big handbags. Thing is I saw one on the television recently. It was Posh Spice, or maybe the Duchess of Cambridge. Someone like that anyway. She had one just like it and I thought 'Oh well somebody's got plenty of money.' But she was struggling with it, you see."

"Struggling with the bag."

"Yes, trying to stop it going on the floor, in the rain. Her hair was long, and it was getting in her face and she was just making a complete pig's ear of the whole thing."

Charlie scratched his head, glanced at Kate. Mrs Brett caught the look between them. Realised that her worth as a witness was coming under scrutiny.

She took a breath. "I'm not explaining this properly. You see she was kneeling on the floor, well not kneeling exactly, sort of crouching."

"Crouching?" Charlie shook his head, not understanding, "Was she ill, or... I mean, could you say why she was crouching on the floor?"

"Well, I can't be sure, but I think there was something wrong with her car. She was at the back, by the boot, you know. Crouching on the floor and sort leaning underneath, groping around by the wheel. That was when I noticed the handbag and I watched her. I thought, well, if that was my bag I would have put it inside. It was leather."

"Right." Charlie nodded at the woman, waiting, hoping for something more.

"Anyway, then the man came," she continued.

This was it. This was it.

"A man. You saw her with someone?"

"Oh yes, he came up and talked to her for a bit. Then she stood up, he collected the things from the top of the car and they walked off together. I thought they were probably just going inside to eat their picnic, instead of in the car you know."

"Did you get a good look at him, this man?"

The woman shook her head, then screwed up her face, "Well, not a really good look. It was raining, the windscreen was wet, you know? He had his back to me, his head down, talking to her."

"How tall was he, can you give us an estimate?" Kate asked.

Mrs Brett pointed at Charlie, "A bit smaller than him, a bit fatter I think and, excuse me, no offence, he wasn't coloured. He was white."

"Did she seem happy to go with him? Did she seem upset?"

"No, as I say she just walked away with him, over towards the parking by the hotel. He carried her shopping and they were talking as they went."

Charlie leaned forward, "Can you tell us anything at all about him? What he was wearing perhaps?"

"Oh, you know, just the usual stuff: dark trousers, I think, a dark jacket. He didn't have a hat because I remember I saw him wipe his hand through his hair, that's how I know he wasn't coloured." She stopped and closed her eyes, "Yes, that was it. A bit heavier than you, not fat, just, you know... bulkier and I'm sorry but that's all I can remember."

"You've been a great help, Mrs Brett," Kate said.

"Well, I hope you find her."

"Thank you. Now, are you alright for getting home?"

"Oh yes, I came here in my car, followed the police one."

Charlie smiled at her, "If you can spare the time we'd like you to give us a written statement, just so we have a proper record for the files. We can come to your home to do it later, if that's more convenient."

"No, it's fine I can do it now."

They left her in the lounge. Another cup of tea and a couple of biscuits seemed like a small reward, but it was all they had to offer and in truth, they knew that recounting this to her local book club, the WI, or whatever, more than made up for the poor refreshments on offer.

* * *

"Noticed the handbag, noticed the hair, but hardly anything about the bloke. Isn't that a bit odd?" Charlie glanced down at Kate as he spoke.

"No, not really, it's a girl thing. You wouldn't understand. But look at what she did give us: shorter than you, Charlie, white, a bit chunkier. Are you thinking the same as me?"

"Well, it does describe Steven Blakely pretty well doesn't it?"

"Let's go and see him again. See what he was wearing on Thursday."

Chapter 9

They were prepared for his reaction when they asked him about his movements; the knack was deciding how genuine it was. When they questioned him again about just what he had done in the minutes before Sarah had been seen talking to someone near the car, they had expected him to be defensive.

Charlie tried to calm him, "We need to form the clearest idea of what happened. Someone saw a woman, they think might have been your partner, talking to a man who could fit your description. All we're trying to do is make sure that we have the series of events clear and concise." They watched his face. Something made Steve's eyes narrow, his skin flush. Was it anger, fear, maybe even guilt? It was hard to decide.

He had a dark jacket, who didn't – he'd shrugged his shoulders as he made the comment, no it wasn't black it was dark brown. In his mind Charlie imagined a brown jacket, rain spotted and darkened, seen through a misted windscreen. He had to tread carefully, if they wanted to take his clothes away, look for mud splatters, evidence of walking in woodland, then they needed more than this.

He had brought Kate with him, she had been in on the interview after all. She leaned forward, spoke quietly, "The woman we brought in said that she had particularly noticed a handbag. It was this apparently that had caught her attention."

Steven Blakely didn't speak. Kate continued, "Does Sarah have a big bag, something a bit special, maybe that another woman would notice?"

When he nodded, Charlie asked the next, obvious question, "Did she have it with her at the services?"

"Yeah. She was thrilled with it. I told her it was totally impractical for the Lakes, you need something like a backpack, something that can put up with the weather, but she insisted. She said that at least she could use it for going there and back." He bent his head, covered his eyes with his hands. "She was so bloody chuffed with it. All I did was sulk, because she'd spent a lot of money. God, what a jerk."

There was nothing they could say. Charlie caught Kate's attention, nodded his head towards the door. She began to gather her things.

Back in the car Charlie spoke quietly. "I don't see it, do you? I just can't see him doing anything to her. He's in bits." He thought for a moment. "I know, it could be a good act, it could be remorse, but…"

"So, we're not taking him in for questioning? Not looking at his clothes?"

"Not unless you really feel strongly about it, Kate, or saw something that I didn't – not for the moment." She shook her head. "I suppose we know where he is, the FLO has her eye on him. Tell you what though, he was right about one thing."

"What's that?"

"Well, there he was giving her grief about spending on the bag, and now look. See, that's what I keep telling my girls. You have to remember that none of us know how long we've got."

"Yes, I think I'm much more aware of that since our baby was born, I want to be there for him, it adds another level of worry somehow."

He had spoken the truth but also knew that you couldn't let it get to you, you couldn't do the job if you let the darkness take over but, through the joking, the banter, they both knew that the longer they went with no real luck, no more hints at what might have happened, the deeper the darkness became.

* * *

The team were in the office when they arrived, no news, nothing to help. There was an air of dullness. Since the excitement of the witness, nothing else was happening. They knew that Sarah had walked away with someone, it was valuable information but that was it. A woman was missing, they had a broken phone, a possible sighting. When you got right down to it that wasn't a lot.

Maybe after the appeal on the television something would break. Charlie gave them the option of staying to help man the phones, along with the CIOs or going home. They all opted to stay. It pleased him, but they would be busy the next day interviewing anyone who genuinely seemed to have information. They needed to be rested, needed to get away and think about something else. "Okay but don't stay too long." They knew, and he knew that they knew, he would be there for as long as he could still function. He spent the time until the broadcast looking at the picture of the blond, pretty young woman with laughter in her eyes, going over and over the little that they had and beginning to acknowledge deep down that this probably wasn't going to end well.

The first bulletin went out at eight, Steven Blakely hollow-eyed, his voice breaking on the plea to just not hurt her, just let her come home, he needed her. He shocked them all when, towards the end he asked her to marry him. It was heart-breaking.

At ten, Charlie went home, dissatisfied, worried and frustrated. Carol was already in bed so he spent another hour staring at the service area on Google earth, memorising every detail although he knew that it wasn't getting him anywhere. He really should get some sleep before the baby had them up again. He was exhausted.

* * *

By the time Charlie arrived next morning, the office was buzzing. The phones were alive, the team engaged, typing, talking. It was a better atmosphere than the day before, they had something to do and it had lifted them.

Reports were on his desk, he shuffled them as he gulped down the strong, black coffee, and rubbed at his eyes.

"Bad night?" Sue stood in the doorway smiling sympathetically. "We've had a decent response, Steve was very compelling."

"Fingers crossed, eh. I really need something to take to the Chief Inspector. I don't want him taking this away and you know, more than that – to be honest…" he paused, didn't want to look weak but then continued, his voice subdued, "I really would like to find her. I know that the longer she's missing the less chance there is of solving this, but I really would like to know she's safe."

She smiled and nodded her head, *he was lovely, wasn't he?*

Chapter 10

The services at Warwick were manic. Apart from the homegoing weekenders, the usual gangs of bikers, ramblers, caravanners and the rest of it, there were the end of week tour groups. Millie and Sonia hefted their suitcases into the café. They flopped into the white plastic chairs beside the window. They were tired, grubby and miserable.

The holiday had been great, the food in France, the wine, the weather brilliant. The journey back, not so much.

"Next time we're gonna fly, Millie." Sonia Tranter held up a hand, "Look, I know you say you don't like it, but come on, you can't like this. If we'd flown we'd have been home by now, your brother would have had a quick trip to the airport to pick us up, job done. Now we have to wait for him to drive down, come across from the other side and then all the way back again. I feel filthy, my feet are swollen from sitting on that bloody coach and I'm still queasy from the ferry. You can get some help, you know, get hypnotised or something. Really, next time, we're flying."

Her friend glared at her, "Yeah – okay. I know, I feel just as grungy, but I hate flying. You've been whinging for the last two hours. Give it a rest, will you? Carl's on his way though. Should be about an hour, we'll be able to see him from here. He'll text when he's a few minutes away and then we'll keep an eye out. Let's get a cup of coffee and chill for a bit. Chill!"

"Right, I'm going to the toilet. I'll pick up some coffee on the way back."

Millie didn't answer, she made a show of gathering the luggage nearer, scraped her chair close to the table and threw herself onto the hard plastic seat. "Yeah. I'll stay here with the bags."

She stared out of the window, her friend was probably right, it was silly. But she hated flying. It wasn't really that she thought they would crash, though that was always a little niggle in the back of her mind. It was the stale air, the closeness of other people, skimpy seats. Maybe one day, when she had the money and could go first class she'd give it a go, but no – Sonia could moan all she wanted, she wasn't flying on a cheap airline. She glared around the restaurant, she was tired and grumpy and wondered if it had been worth the bother of going away at all. She pulled her hair away from her face, twined it around her hand and stuck it up in a messy bun.

She was aware of the person beside the table before he spoke. She turned, looked up.

She glanced around for Sonia, but there was no sign of her mate. "Yes, can I help you?"

In response he smiled down at her, held out his wallet. It was a black folder, on one side was his picture, she glanced up, yes that was him. On the other side was a badge of some sort.

She shrugged, waited for him to speak.

"I'm sorry to bother you." She raised her eyebrows. "I noticed you sitting here. Have you seen the posters?" As he spoke he indicated the pictures on a couple of the pillars. She hadn't noticed them particularly but wasn't about to say so. She didn't speak, left it to him. She just wanted him to go away, she wasn't going to buy anything. She was aware that she was glaring, she didn't care.

"We're looking for a young woman. She disappeared from one of the service areas a few days ago." He showed her one of the posters, she glanced at it quickly, took in the basic facts.

She really couldn't be bothered with this, "I've just come back from France. Can't help you, sorry."

He leaned a little closer, "It's just that she looked very like you."

"Oh well, as I say I've just come back from France, so it's not me."

"Thing is, we are looking for someone to do a reconstruction. Try to jog people's memories, that sort of thing. We would film it for the television. It would only take a bit of time, an hour maybe. Do you think you could help us out?"

"Don't you use actresses for that stuff?"

He shook his head, "No, not really. Sometimes we use our own people, but quite often it's a friend, a relative or just someone who looks really like the subject. You're the right height and build, your hair's right." He reached a hand forward, pointed at her head. "I noticed it just before you tied it up. We'd give you the clothes, to make you look like her. Not her clothes obviously, similar to what she was wearing. It really would be a huge help."

Where the hell was Sonia? She glanced around again, there was still no sign. "I have to watch the bags till my mate comes back. I was going to have a cup of coffee."

"Oh, that's not a problem. I can have someone come in, sit with the luggage, explain to your friend. He waved a hand in the direction of a couple of policemen in uniform. "We've got coffee in the van."

What should she do? If one of her friends was missing she'd want to help. This was someone's daughter, maybe even someone's wife. "Oh, okay then. What do you want me to do?"

"I'll get someone to come and take care of the bags."
He turned away, murmured into his phone. "Right, that's sorted. We really do appreciate this. If you'd just come with me. The van's outside."

"Oh, no hang on. I'm not going off somewhere."

"It's just the van, the one we're using as a base you know. It's only over there." He waved a hand in the direction of the motel.

"Okay then. But, if she went missing from Cherwell Valley, why are you doing it here?"

"Just in case someone stopped there on Friday but is here today, people don't always use the same services. You'll just need to walk around while we make an announcement. You look so much like her. It really might be a breakthrough for us if someone remembers seeing her. Someone else is doing it at the other services. We haven't been able to find anyone here that looks as much like her as you do."

She slid out from behind the table and, still unsure, still puzzled, still looking around for Sonia, she followed him out to the car park.

Chapter 11

Sometimes you just know.

When the phone vibrated, and it was still dark outside, the gap around the windows not yet lined with a bit of brightness, the blackbird yet to start his early morning warbling, Charlie groaned. He didn't look at the clock. It didn't matter what time it was, the main thing was not disturbing the baby.

It was the control room. "Sorry Charlie. We thought you'd want to know. There's another woman missing."

"Bugger. What do we know?" He was awake now, wide awake, already kicking the duvet away, already juggling with the phone and the T-shirt, moving quickly and quietly towards the door.

"M40. Woman went to the toilets, left her friend looking after their bags, waiting for a lift. When she came back there was a uniform with the bags, just about to start an unaccompanied bags incident, no sign of her mate. No answer on her phone, no reason for her to have gone anywhere."

"Thanks. I'll get down there. Look, could you get in touch with Sue Bakshi, tell her I'll pick her up at the station in about..." He glanced at his watch. "Twenty minutes?"

He splashed cold water on his face, crept back into the bedroom to grab his clothes. He peeped into the crib, Joshua was fast asleep. "I've got to go out love," Carol opened her eyes and frowned at him. "I'll ring you later. Go back to sleep. Baby's fine."

He slid on his shoes and then remembered the last place where the phone had been found: dog muck, mud. He pulled a pair of old wellies from the shelf in the utility room, stowed them in the car boot, threw on a gilet. There was the blackbird, oh well, not quite the middle of the night then.

* * *

Although they never completely closed, the services were almost empty, the outlets were locked and dark, it felt cold. In the corner of the quiet cafeteria a small group huddled round a table littered with disposable cups and tissues. There were a couple of uniformed officers sitting beside a young woman who was huddled under a coat which was obviously too big for her. Beside her a young man in T-shirt and jeans was wringing his hands together, occasionally lifting his mobile phone from the table, clicking buttons, tossing it back among the detritus.

Charlie joined them, introduced himself and Sue.

The man looked up, glanced at them, "What are you here for then? What's happening? My sister's missing and it seems to me that nobody's doing anything. We've told these people everything we know. We've hung around and hung around, first the manager of this place, then their security, now you. When is somebody actually going to do something?" He pointed a finger in the direction of a young man in a crumpled looking suit, his phone clutched in his hand like a shield, hair dishevelled and greasy. "He said we should just go home. Just go home when we've no idea where Millie is. Bloody idiot."

Charlie held up a hand, nodded to the manager who managed a tight smile. He was out of his depth and confused.

One of the uniformed constables spoke quietly, calmly. "This is Carl Roberts. His sister was here with Sonia. They were just coming back from a holiday in France. Left by the coach at just after eight this evening. While Sonia here was in the toilets, her friend, Carl's sister, Millie – Millicent – was looking after the bags. When Sonia came back, Millie was gone. No response to her phone since then and no reason that she should have left."

"Thanks." Charlie had known all of this from the phone conversation he'd had with the dispatcher on the way to pick up Sue, but understood the other officer was simply trying to reassure the relatives and the friend that they had it all noted, they were in control, they had been listened to.

* * *

It was emotional, they tried to keep the situation calm but it was obvious this time that there was something wrong. "Have we looked at the CCTV yet?" he addressed the officer who had just spoken, the older of the two, the one who had taken charge until now.

"They've taken the recordings away, I think we've got something. I don't know how much use it will be, but you never know."

"Great." Charlie leaned across the table, "Mr Roberts. We are going to do all we can to find your sister. It might well turn out to be nothing to worry about. Maybe she met a friend, something like that. Usually there's a simple explanation." They didn't believe him, it was obvious, and he didn't believe himself. Not for a minute. "I will get someone to go home with you now. What about you, Sonia, have you someone waiting for you?"

"My mum. I live with my mum. We had a bit of a row, me and Millie. She was miffed with me, we were both tired and stressed. But she wouldn't just have gone off, she

49

just wouldn't." She tried to hold back tears, but they overflowed and rolled down her cheeks to be wiped away with trembling hands.

"Okay, look, what I'd like is for you all to go and get some rest, this has been a long and difficult night for you. I'll arrange for someone to come and speak to you later today. In the meantime, if we find out anything we'll let you know immediately. Honestly, the best thing now is for you to be at home. In case Millie tries to contact you. In case she turns up."

"You know something we don't," said the brother, straighter now in his chair, suspicion in his eyes. "What is this all about?"

"We don't know anything yet. It's too early. We are just worried, as you are. From what you've said, there was no reason for Millie to go missing, we are taking this seriously. If I hear anything I will let you know personally."

There was no way becoming involved in a heated back and forth would accomplish anything so, with a nod to the uniforms, Charlie turned to Sue, flicked a glance towards the door, stood and walked out.

When she joined him a few minutes later she confirmed they had arranged escorts for them all to go home and for members from the team to visit them after lunch to take official statements and bring back recent pictures and anything else that might help.

"Bloody hell, Charlie. What is this?" She didn't expect an answer.

Chapter 12

When the call came from Bob Scunthorpe's office Charlie had been expecting it, really just waiting to be called in, and he knew it wasn't going to be for congratulations. He had his notes prepared and up to date, his plan outlined. He didn't feel out of his depth, but he was frustrated and anxious. Another woman missing, and they were no nearer to tracing the first one. It wasn't good.

Glenys ushered him straight into the office, "Do you want coffee, Detective Inspector?"

He shook his head.

The Chief Inspector stood and came around the desk, shook his hand and then turned to the slim young woman who had also left her seat and taken a couple of paces forward. "Charlie, this is Detective Inspector Miller, Tanya." Charlie saw that she was older than he was, but not by much. Slight but fit looking, long fair hair and blue eyes. Her face was serious. Her grip when she shook his hand was strong. She nodded at him, gave a small smile that was really not much more than a twitch of her lips, then, when Bob Scunthorpe moved back to his seat, she sat down leaving Charlie no real option but to take the other chair. He already knew what was coming.

Bob cleared his throat, "I've read the reports. Another woman missing from the motorway services. We are not having much luck with finding Ms…erm."

Charlie interrupted, "Dickinson, sir. Sarah Dickinson."

"Right. Now I think we can use a bit of help here. This is no reflection on you, Charlie. I promise you that, but Inspector Miller has worked in missing persons, and also been involved in several unlawful deaths recently. I think that she could have a lot to offer. She's been seconded to us from Cheshire, though she worked with us until she was promoted, before your time here. We are short-handed as you know, hah, not that they are any better further north, but…" He stopped and waved a hand in the air over his blotter. "No point getting into that now. Charlie, I'd like you to help her feel at home, work together on this, and see if we can't move things along. Of course, we are all hoping that these women will turn up alive and well but, realistically, that might well not be the case and I don't want to be caught napping. Do you have any questions?"

He had a myriad, his mind swirled with them, but he had to be professional. Charlie swallowed hard. "We'll be sharing an office, will we, sir?"

"I think that's best. You've got room I think?"

"Yes of course. I have to ask, sir, is Inspector Miller taking over the case, what I mean to say is…" He paused, didn't know how to phrase his question.

The Chief Inspector was sympathetic but there was no time for pussy footing, "Detective Miller has seniority. I don't want you to feel in any way that you've been side-lined, but someone has to be in charge and naturally…"

Charlie nodded. "Thank you, sir. Did you want me to update you about the new woman?"

"I have it here thank you, Charlie." He held up a slim file folder, "But, I'm sure Inspector Miller would appreciate a thorough run down of everything." He nodded towards the woman who was already bending to retrieve the leather bag that stood on the floor at her feet.

She stood, ready to take care of business, "I've read the reports already, but yes please, Inspector, that would be useful. Shall we go and get on with it?"

Charlie led the way, past the secretary, out into the corridor. He was struggling, disappointment and anger battling with the overriding attempt to appear unfazed. They walked in silence along the narrow space. Just before they reached the squad room he paused, turned to look down at her, "Do you want to meet the team now, or would you rather get settled in the office first?"

"Let's meet the team, get that bit done. Can I call you Charlie, or would you prefer to keep things formal?" She knew when she asked what the answer had to be, they had to be on first name terms, anything else would be ludicrous.

"Charlie's fine, and you?"

"Tanya." She smiled, "I know you're feeling pretty miffed about this, I would be, but honestly I just want us to find these women. There's no time for turf wars, let's try and make it work?"

Charlie nodded at her and opened the door to the incident room, stood back to let her enter first. He bit back the bile. It wasn't her fault, she had been sent here, probably hadn't had a lot of choice, but it smarted, it really did.

"Okay guys, can I have a minute?" The team looked up, Sue frowned at him, "This is Detective Inspector Miller, Tanya. She's been brought in to give us a hand."

Tanya nodded at them all. "I'm going to be working closely with Charlie, I have some experience that might be useful. It's no reflection on what's been achieved up to now, just more help with this case. It seems that it could be bigger than was first thought. Charlie's sharing his office with me, that'll make things easier we think."

She'd been considerate, he appreciated it, but it still stung. He showed her into the small room in the corner, there was a spare desk. He had taken the bigger one when he'd moved in. He saw her glance at his and then without another word she pulled open the drawer of the smaller one and pushed her handbag inside.

"Right then, let's get on with it shall we?"

They could hear the team in the outside office, could imagine the conversation but there were more important things to discuss than pecking order and Charlie took a deep breath, he'd handle this.

For a while they were stiff, awkward with each other, but as they went through the evidence, discussed options, the atmosphere started to thaw.

After an hour they went back to the incident room for Tanya to address the team about their tasks moving forward. She would need to lay any residual awkwardness to rest quickly, they didn't have time for personality clashes. She would face it head on.

"Okay, I know you're possibly a bit confused about what's going on. Probably you feel a bit miffed, think I've put Charlie's nose out of joint. Please let's just move past that. It's not true, you all have been doing a great job. It's just thought that my particular skill set has something to offer for this situation. Does anyone have anything they want to say? Let's get it out of the way up front."

Nobody said anything for a while and then Sue stood from behind her desk, "So, we're to report to you now, are we?"

"Charlie and I are sharing an office, we'll be working together. If I'm not there, then of course anything you need to share can come through Charlie. Is that clear?"

The younger woman nodded, sat down and began fiddling with the papers on her desk. Tanya turned and walked out of the room, back to the office.

Charlie followed her. This had happened, it was time to get back to work.

Chapter 13

Tanya left Bob Scunthorpe's office and stalked to her own, smaller, shared one, flopped onto her desk chair, and let out a huge gust of a sigh.

Charlie moved over to the table in the corner, switched on the kettle and spooned instant coffee into two mugs.

"Well that could have been worse." She smiled at him as he handed her the drink. He managed to grin back at her.

"Right. Apparently, the new woman's family want a televised appeal, the Chief Inspector is not happy, he feels it takes the attention away from Sarah and she's been missing longer, arguably it's more urgent that we find her, though of course they both matter just as much. It doesn't look good does it? One so soon after the other, so similar. That's the other thing, the panic. We don't want to start people talking about serial abduction, well we don't want people to talk about anything much until we get a better idea of what's going on, except the ones who have something useful to say. The second girl, Millie, she disappeared from a place crawling with coppers. How the hell did that happen?" She sipped at the drink, "Yuck. I need my sugar on a day like this." She stirred in a heaped spoonful and took a big gulp. "It's possible, isn't it, Charlie, that they're not connected. Just coincidence. Two women?" She stopped when she saw the look on his face, no way he thought it was coincidence, neither did she.

The reports the team brought in during the next couple of hours told them nothing new, not yet. The CCTV footage was still being examined, the services staff who had been on duty the day before had been questioned. Nobody had seen anything happen, nobody had been aware of a woman in distress, no struggle, no argument.

"She went voluntarily, didn't she?" Tanya swung round on her desk chair. "Millie just went off. So, did she go on her own or did she meet someone. Let's go next door, Charlie, see how things are going with the video. It was inside, we've got to have it recorded."

Before they had the chance to move, the door opened, it was Sue, she took a step towards Charlie. Tanya held out a hand. "Thanks, what's this?"

"Screen grab from the vid. We can see Millie at the table and someone, a man, talking to her. You might want to come through and watch though. She goes off with him no problem. She doesn't look entirely happy, but she just gets up and goes out."

They gathered around the monitor in the incident room. All of them, leaning in to get a closer view. They ran the short sequence again.

Charlie turned away, took the print out and pinned it on the new board they had set up. On the top was Millie's holiday face grinning down at them, tanned and happy.

"Right," Tanya waved a hand towards the computer as the image froze. Two people walking away from the table, out towards the car park where they had seen film of them rapidly disappearing around the corner of the building, behind the walls of the hotel. "So, that's it then. She chose to go with that bloke. I mean he didn't touch her, not even a hand on her arm. What else, what do you see, people?"

"It was a relatively long conversation for a stranger." As DS Paul Harris spoke, Tanya nodded.

"Yes, more than just 'hello, are you on your own?' There was quite a back and forth. What else?" Nobody answered; were they hesitating because they weren't at ease yet? There had already been enough time for them to become a team. She had to find a way to get them to work with her at the head and there wasn't time to just let it build.

Charlie was speaking, filling the silence. "She seemed comfortable, not stressed but not exactly friendly. I don't think she knew him."

"He uses his phone doesn't he, just before she gets up to go with him." Sue spoke this time.

"Yes, and there's that other thing." Paul waved a hand towards the screen. "He shows her something. If you wind it back, you can see they are both looking down at something in his hand. Is that his phone or something else?"

"Can we zoom in on that?"

They leaned closer, played the sequence again.

"Shit," Paul muttered. None of the others spoke. Sue reached into her pocket, dragged out the wallet holding her warrant card, held it up.

"Nah, it can't be." Charlie said, shaking his head.

Tanya's throat had dried, this couldn't be happening, it was the stuff of nightmares. No way this could be one of them, someone on the job.

She crossed her arms in front of her, "Hold on, I know what that looks like but let's not get ahead of ourselves. There are lots of other jobs, lots of other situations where that happens." She stopped, she knew it was true but for the life of her she couldn't name one right then.

Sue spoke up again, she was readier than the others to put herself forward, risk being noticed. Tanya knew that she had been working closely with Charlie; maybe she was finding it hard to relinquish that small feeling of being favoured. She understood, if you didn't work at it then you fell by the wayside, especially as a woman, even today. She nodded as Sue voiced her thoughts, "It could be a civilian."

"Yes, carry on."

"Well I was just thinking, charity workers, those people who are deaf, trying to sell you something, they have i.d. don't they?"

A couple of the group nodded, "Check with the services, see if they'd approved anyone like that. More, give me more."

"Security." This was Dan. "The services have their own security don't they, they'd have i.d., and the parking people? Even the AA and RAC guys touting for business by the doors, they would have a card."

It felt like movement, a step forward but as she asked for print outs of the two of them talking at the table, arranged for copies to be emailed to the services, the HR department, she knew, they all knew, the image they had seen had been so familiar, they all did it all the time. Introduced themselves, showed their i.d. It was second nature, they didn't even think about it.

As they left the incident room she leaned in to whisper to Charlie, "Tell me this isn't what it looked like, Charlie."

"No, course not." He didn't sound convinced.

Chapter 14

She was playing catch up, coming in when things had already happened, Tanya had to become familiar with it all, until she knew as much as the rest of the team. She'd gone over the paperwork again, looked at the stills, been through and run the video. In the incident room everyone was still fielding calls from the appeal for information about Sarah Dickinson. There was nothing. Nothing to take them any nearer. Sue's call to the service area management had brought up no charity workers, not ones there with approval anyway. She'd reached out and asked for details of all the police personnel who would have been at the services for the hour before and after the time that Millie and her friend were dropped off, whether they were involved in the search for Sarah or not.

At some point she would have to go through and tell Bob Scunthorpe what they thought they had seen. Before then she wanted to turn over every stone in the hope that she could say she didn't think it was an officer. Right now though, she couldn't. They had enhanced the image as much as possible and it hadn't helped to set their minds at rest. The thing in his hand looked like a warrant card, even the way he had flipped it open had been familiar. He was clever about the cameras, they still had no clear image of his face.

The office door opened, she looked up. "Kate, what have you got?"

"I did a quick Google search and, well I don't know whether this is good news or not, but you can buy warrant cards on line."

"What? You're kidding me."

"I wish I was, but no. It was really easy, they are memorabilia things, for fans of cop shows and for theatre props, you can get lanyards as well, they look pretty convincing, the badge and all. It would be no problem for someone with a bit of skill with an imaging programme to put their own picture in there. You could probably even use something like your driving licence. Thing is, the general public, unless they have dealings with us regularly, would they have a clue? I mean if you've never seen one before, if you were taken by surprise say, or just not on your guard, maybe a bit embarrassed. Well, I reckon you'd be fooled. He took it out of his pocket, gave her a quick look and then away again."

Tanya pursed her lips, Charlie had joined them at the desk. He spoke, "So, if that's the case then this low life is deliberately going out to fool women into thinking he's official. That's why they go with him."

"If that's what he's done maybe we could find out who's bought them." Even as Tanya said it she knew it was impossible. They would never have the manpower to do that sort of search, starting from nothing, and Morse, Lewis, Frost, well there were fans world-wide, any of whom would possibly like an imitation warrant card. She shook her head. The policewoman was turning away, her shoulders slumped, "That was a good thought though, Kate, it gives us more information and at least I can tell the Chief Inspector that it's very possible it's not someone in the force."

* * *

60

There was protocol to follow and tried and tested routines, Tanya had done all that she could, she had been over everything. There was nothing to show for her first day. The trail was going cold, the chance of solving this would slip away quickly. She poked her head round the door of the incident room, told them all to wind up what they were doing, get some rest. Maybe tomorrow would give them a breakthrough. Hey, maybe tomorrow the women would turn up alive and well. Nobody looked convinced.

Charlie met her in the corridor, she looked up at him, "So, you've got a new baby? That must be hard, on top of all this?"

He nodded at her. "Actually, I could do with an afternoon off tomorrow, well a couple of hours anyway, any chance? Carol wants to go out with her sister. She hasn't been very well and I'm trying to help as much as I can. It's rotten timing I know but I'll make the time up and come back if anything breaks."

"Well, unless something happens tomorrow I can't see why not."

She thought about him as she drove home. She'd felt sorry for him, but he'd handled himself well. She thought of him telling his wife about the new woman brought in above him. That would be difficult. What would it be like? What did it feel like to have someone at home, someone waiting to hear about your day? Someone who knew all about you. Tanya had nobody anymore, not really. Her sister lived in Scotland, they never did get on anyway, mum and dad were gone, and she'd never had aunties, grandparents. What would that be like? And babies, what was that all about, with the pressure of this job, was it worth it? Why would someone inflict that on themselves?

She didn't like babies, not much, didn't see the attraction. She'd never been able to understand the whole business of having an heir, someone to carry on the name. It's not as if Charlie and Carol were royalty, there was nothing for little Joshua to inherit, except maybe if he was lucky a semi in Oxford and a second-hand car. It just wasn't worth all the stress. Not for her, no. Not even if she did meet someone she might want to be with for a while, nothing about this whole baby business was attractive.

There was a lasagne waiting for her, a couple of glasses of wine and then a Game of Thrones dvd. Her little house on the outskirts of Oxford was cosy. It was her haven. Her dad had left her money, shared between the two of them. More for her sister, supposedly because she had children but, whatever, it had been enough for a decent deposit, so the mortgage was manageable. She'd rented it out while she was posted away, but once she knew she was coming back she'd had it cleaned, got herself a woman to come in regularly. She was happy to be home, hoped that maybe it could be for a while. She didn't feel lonely, never, but still, what would it be like sharing her space? She couldn't imagine it now, it had been too long.

She closed the door behind her, paused for a minute, listening to the quiet; breathing in the faint scent from the diffuser wands in the hall. There was a small white card on the table by the door. "Sod it." The delivery was supposed to have been in the afternoon, she had stated it on the order so Mrs Green would be there to receive it. Since when was nine thirty, afternoon? Now, she'd have to go and collect it. She sighed, she was going to start having stuff delivered to work. The trouble with that though was everyone would know. It wasn't that her shopping was unreasonable, she spoiled herself now and then, that was all. Well, she worked hard, she had no-one else to consider and, all things being equal she'd have a decent pension when she retired. She was going to make it to Assistant Chief Constable, maybe higher, maybe all the way to the top; then she'd be set up for the rest of her life, so why not spend what she wanted to. She needed decent clothes for work after all, needed to make the right impression.

She pushed the card into the pocket on the back of her bag, walked through to the kitchen and turned on the oven.

Chapter 15

The next morning Tanya was in the office early, the team all poked their heads around the door to say good morning; all except Sue. She made a point of giving her a smile as she walked into the incident room. She gave them time to grab a cup of coffee or whatever it was they did to mark the start of the day. Everyone had something, even if was only taking off their outside clothes and draping jackets on the back of the chair.

"Okay – today the main thing is to find a connection between these two women. You all know the statistics. Victims are usually known to their attackers. I know we didn't see an 'attack'," Tanya waved quote marks in the air with her fingers. "But we must assume the same person has taken them and his intentions are evil. So, is there a connection? Look at schools, colleges, friends, gyms, shop loyalty cards, anything you can think of. For the moment I think we should all concentrate on that. We've still got bods on the ground at both service areas so that's covered. Sue, can you co-ordinate it?" The special attention won her a grudging smile, she needed a friend in the ranks, but this young woman probably wasn't going to be the one. "Paul, will you make sure they are both featured on the website,

Facebook page and Twitter. Be a bit careful, I don't want them linked in the public mind yet, not until we're sure. At the moment they are just two separate missing women." As she spoke he typed notes into his tablet, nodded, pushed his glasses up on his nose, that was a particular habit of his.

She was getting to know the team quickly, trying to judge what might be their strengths and weaknesses. She stood from where she had leaned her hip on the corner of the desk, and gathered her things, "Me and Charlie are going back to see Steven Blakely, we need to let him know we are still on this. Then I'm going to talk to Millie's mum and dad. All calls to me this afternoon. Charlie's off doing other stuff."

As they went back to their office Tanya spoke to Charlie, "I think they're starting to accept what happened, aren't they? Have you got used to the idea? I really appreciate the way you handled yesterday, it can't have been easy."

They were in the office gathering their clothes and bags, shutting down the computers.

"Yeah, well no point dwelling on stuff, is there? You've got things to offer. I won't pretend I wasn't a bit put out, but to be honest I wasn't completely surprised. We're stretched too thin, everywhere, it's not like it used to be with teams together for years."

"Tell me about it." She sighed, scrubbed at her scalp, easing the tension. "Will it be today, Charlie, will we get a break today? It's as if we still don't even know what we are looking at. Is it abduction? Will there be some sort of demand, or is it all something darker? If it is and we don't find something soon it's all going to go horribly pear shaped, isn't it? The longer it goes on with no contact, nothing, the more that seems likely. These poor women."

"Something's going to come up soon. I wondered about a reconstruction."

"It's on the cards for Sarah. Next Friday if we are still no further on, there's a chance some of the regulars at the services will remember something."

"Oh right. I didn't know."

"Sorry, I arranged it first thing."

"Right, I see. Are you sure it's okay for me to take this afternoon off?"

"Yeah, with a bit of luck we'll find something today and then you'll be too busy chasing bad guys to go swanning off playing happy families."

With a glance back at the building, at the light shining in the incident room window and the movement of figures behind the glass, she shook her head, and muttered under her breath, "Come on guys, find me something."

* * *

They had expected the interview with Steven Blakely to be difficult, but Charlie was surprised, yet again, by his deterioration. He'd lost weight, his face was unshaven, haggard looking. The liaison officer said that he was hardly eating.

Tanya wished she'd been able to avoid coming but it was the right thing to do. She had nothing of any substance to tell him, nothing to give him any hope but she needed to show her face, introduce herself. They went over old ground, he had found some more pictures, recent trips and holidays. Though they didn't see what good they would be, they didn't have the heart to say so, and they took the prints away with them.

"He's really going to pieces. Meeting him for the first time, what do you reckon?" Charlie leaned on the car, talking through the window.

"It's awful isn't it? I can see he's falling apart, and we can't offer him anything."

"Do you think it's a bit intense? I know she's missing, I know it's scary and worrying and all that but right from the start he's been like this. The very first time we met him, he was a wreck."

"What are you saying, Charlie?"

"I reckon we should look a bit more closely. Maybe have another word with some of their friends, see just how tight they were. You know, just see if there was any suggestion of trouble, any girl talk over a bottle of wine, that sort of thing."

"Can't do any harm I suppose. Why don't you get on that tomorrow? A bit discrete though, don't forget how all this started, him ranting on the internet. I understand that he's keeping off at the moment and I prefer it that way and Bob Scunthorpe does as well."

They split up, Tanya to go and make herself known to Millie's distraught and frantic parents, and Charlie to go and have a bit of light relief with his son.

It was four o'clock in the afternoon when the call came in. If the day had been sunny, if it had been more like September than November, there would have been more people about, more walkers, more visitors to the country church and it would have come sooner, but when the phone burbled, and she clicked the hands free on the steering wheel, Tanya's stomach flipped.

Sometimes you just know.

Chapter 16

Station road was lined with cars that had been pulled onto the grass verge beside St Mary's Church, churning up the mud. Crime scene tape was stretched through the crossroads behind the churchyard. Although there was a low stone wall around the area, they had cars on the roads. Just now, there weren't many people about in the dull, drizzling rain, but once word got out there would be dozens, drawn by the drama. It wasn't possible to avoid it, so it had to be managed, as best they could.

A safe path had been marked out with a uniformed officer posted at the gap that formed a gateway leading to the narrow tarmac path.

Tanya pulled on the shoe covers, gloves, the suit and tucked her hair up inside her hood. She made her way round the end of the old building and into the graveyard. The pop-up plastic cover was already there. Suited figures moved quietly on the mounded grass, faceless and spectral between the old graves in the fading, grey light. Out beyond the wall the mortuary van waited.

It was a very English church, ancient and plain with just some fancy stonework round the windows and doors. Grey stone walls, a dark slate roof, merging with the miserable day. It had probably featured in hundreds of wedding albums, christening pictures, happy days, precious memories and now it was tainted, spoiled by wickedness.

Tanya moved on, she didn't want this to be Sarah Dickinson, Millie Roberts, she didn't want to take this news to Steve, worried and wasting away in his silent flat. She didn't want to go back to Millie's parents with the worst news she could bring them. But then, she didn't want it to be anyone, didn't want any family torn apart and plunged into such grief. There was nothing she could do about it except to find the reasons, search out the explanations and find the monster who had left a young woman's body draped across a grave in an old English churchyard.

She called Charlie, but his phone was off – not surprising if he was in sole charge of the baby, and it might be his last chance for a while. She left a message, asked him to meet her there in Ardley. Told him that they may have had the breakthrough, but that it was the worst possible thing.

She had to pull back the plastic to gain access so when she turned to the scene it hit her full in the face. She had expected to see a body, probably blood, possibly lots of blood, maybe something worse. There was none of it.

Because of the dimness, they had brought in floodlights, which caught the shine and gleam of jewels. They turned the white gown into a living shimmering thing, glowing against the dark stone slab. For a moment Tanya was speechless, breathless. For just a brief while it was astonishing, an ethereal figure, pale hands crossed on her breast, long blond hair cascading towards the wet grass. Like something from a fantasy film.

Then the medical examiner spoke and the moment broke, reality hit her, and the brutality stole away the magic.

A tall figure, covered in protective clothing, leaning over a medical bag, unfolded to his full height, well over six feet, and nodded at Tanya. She held up her warrant card. "Hello Detective Inspector, Dr Hewitt – Simon. I believe this young woman may be one of yours." He waved a gloved hand towards the body.

Tanya leaned closer, she already knew. "Yes, I'm afraid so. Can you tell me anything?"

"Not much as yet. She hasn't been here very long I don't think. This rain has been coming down since first thing so everywhere is soaking and that doesn't help us. I've only just arrived really, it's taken us a while to get all this organised…" He raised his hand to indicate the plastic walls and roof. "Haven't moved her much yet so you are getting the full experience. As is obvious, she has been posed, prepared – look." He lifted up the slender hand. "Her nails have been painted, she has make up on."

"What's the smell? Something faint?"

"Yes, it was probably a lot stronger before the rain got to it. Bleach I'm afraid. So, she's been washed and the clothes as well I imagine. I don't think we're going to get anything much in the way of residues, dust, whatever."

"What killed her."

"Ah. Well now. I'm not going to say. I have an idea, but I would rather wait until I have her back in our place. I will let you know as soon as I can, I'll call you, but no I'm not going to guess and really, it's not going to matter much, if it is what I think."

"How do you mean it won't matter?"

He turned away. "No, please just have a little patience."

"We have another woman missing."

He stood straight, she could tell by the creases around his eyes that he had grimaced, "I'm sorry to hear that. I really am. I will get back to you as quickly as I can. In the meantime, all I can do is ask for your patience."

Tanya thanked him, turned and ducked back out into the graveyard. Charlie was making his way towards her over the grass, dodging between the graves. She waved to him, a sad, small acknowledgement. She was thankful for the wet weather disguising the moisture on her cheeks.

Chapter 17

Tanya went with Charlie to see Steven Blakely. The whole thing was hideous. He railed at them, sobbed, threatened, and then collapsed into his chair, his head buried in his hands, groaning and shaking, murmuring her name. Sarah would only just have been taken to the mortuary, and there was work to be done before he could see her. They would take him the next day, he was incapable right then and anyway, they knew it was her. There would have to be a formal identification, but the ring and bracelet they had brought with them, in plastic evidence bags, had been enough to destroy him.

Just as they arrived at the office, the Liaison Officer called to say that they had needed the doctor and he was now under sedation.

Tanya thought about her own parents, her mother slowly slipping away within a year after her father had died. Then there was her sister: one drama after the other with her kids until in the end it was all too tedious, and she stopped asking, just didn't bother anymore. It wasn't worth it, better by far to keep to yourself, live your own life, no partner, no kids, no pain.

* * *

The mood in the incident room was sombre. It was after nine o'clock. They'd stayed late, though Tanya told them that if they needed to get home, there wouldn't be much more information until the next day and, providing they were contactable, they could leave. Nobody left. Tanya decided she might as well make the most of it, start the meeting she had planned for early morning.

Charlie pinned the pictures on the board – the body, the church, the graves – for a minute nobody said anything. Tanya let them settle, take in the facts: this was murder. Though it had always been on the cards, right from the very first report, while there was a chance, until now, there had been a tiny glimmer of hope.

She leaned against the corner of the desk. Waited for them to turn off phones, grab their drinks, open notebooks and so on. "Right, the SOCO team are pretty much finished on the ground, first formal reports due tomorrow, but I've had a chat on the phone."

"Let's start with what we know. It was wet, and so there was no-one about until the poor old biddy who found the body. There are tyre tracks on the verge near the gate but that may not mean much. There was a wedding yesterday, cars all over the place. The medical examiner reckons that the body and the clothes had been washed in bleach and then left out in the rain for a while; he doesn't think more than a few hours. The verger opened the church doors at seven in the morning and he is sure there was nothing there then, so that gives us a time window."

Sue raised her hand, "We don't have a cause of death yet?"

"No, but I reckon Doctor Hewitt has an idea. He wouldn't share but he promised to give us a call soon as… I haven't worked with him before, anybody else know him?" She glanced around, no-one responded. "Right. Tasks. Starting first thing, Sue, will you get on to trying to find out where that dress came from. It looks expensive, a wedding dress, how hard can that be, they're pretty special aren't they?"

"They're bloody expensive I'll tell you that." Everyone turned to look at Paul, standing near the door. "I got married last year and they cost an arm and a leg. It all does: shoes, cars, flowers, reception. I'll tell you what, by the time you get there you wonder if it's all worth it. Maybe that's it, this is just someone who couldn't take it anymore, the constant wedding, wedding, wedding, every bloody day."

There was a moment of silence broken by Kate, "Aw poor you." He turned and glared at her.

Tanya spoke, diffusing the moment, "Maybe I should put you on tracing the dress then, eh?"

"No thank you. I'll tell you what, after two years of solid wedding talk I don't want to hear about bridal shopping ever again. Anyway, I didn't have anything to do with that, all secret that stuff, supposed to be unlucky for the groom to know about it – load of bunk."

Charlie had been quiet until now, he coughed. "There wasn't any hint that Steve and Sarah were going to get married, before all this I mean?"

Tanya shook her head. "Not until the TV appeal and that surprised us all, seemed like a spur of the moment thing, but I guess we should put it in the mix, it's a good point. You would have thought he'd have said something, there was no engagement ring in the evidence, just this little silver one." She picked up the small plastic bag and turned it to catch the light.

"She wouldn't have the dress though, would she?" Sue said, "I mean if they were so near to a wedding that she actually had the dress he'd have said so, I can't believe he wouldn't. You only get them a week or so before. There's nothing on his Facebook page, or hers, it would have all been there, wouldn't it?"

Paul spoke again, quieter this time, "Could be it's a family thing. My wife's mother kept hers I think. She's got

74

a sister, younger. I think the plan is to use it again. Mind you she'll have to get some of the lard off her backside first." He laughed, but when nobody joined in he lowered his head, embarrassed, and sipped at his coffee.

Tanya wrote a couple of notes on the board, names beside the images, Sue for the dress, Paul for the church. She nodded at him, "Will you make it a priority to find out what you can about the grave? It's old I know, but we need to know who's in it and what have you. Maybe someone's bride is in there, the vicar is expecting someone to come and look at the church records, it might give us a hint. Why was she put there? Why was the body arranged like that? Surely, that's got to tell us something. And there's this."

She held up an evidence bag, jiggling it to catch the light. "It looks like that stuff you put on Christmas trees, what do you call it?"

"Tinsel."

"Thanks Dan, yeah. Tinsel. Apart from the usual stuff, fag ends, bits of paper, dead flower stalks, this was the only thing that was a bit out of the ordinary."

"Where was it?" Kate stood and leaned over her desk to have a closer look.

Tanya turned to look at Kate as she spoke, "It was near the top of the grave, by the cross. I don't know if that means much, it could simply be a bit of rubbish, but the graveyard is well kept, the grass cut regularly and all that. So, for the moment this is a mystery. There must have been hundreds of weddings over the last few years, but surely not many that go wrong in some way. So, bear that in mind when you speak to the vicar, Paul. We're looking for someone being jilted I guess, anything we can think of going horribly wrong, that might turn someone, make them so bitter that they could do something like this."

She continued, "If we get an idea about how long ago the dress was sold that'll possibly help. It's the only thing we have to go on. What was the reason for him to pick on

Sarah, did he know her – it's likely – we'll have to get a list of recent boyfriends, see if any of them proposed, were turned down and are bitter enough for this. But that doesn't explain Millie. We just need to keep at it until something shakes loose. At the moment anything and everything is worth exploring so don't hold back, any ideas at all, let's share them." Tanya paused and waited for them to answer.

"Something I did think was a bit odd." Sue had walked to the board, she pointed at the close up of the dress laid out on a table in the lab. "I mean, a wedding, it's about the dress, yes, but it's not just that, it's the shoes, the headdress, flowers, garters, all sorts of things. The dress is the main thing I guess, but if you were trying to recreate a bride – well I don't know, wouldn't you do the whole thing, especially the flowers, a veil perhaps? They've spent some time haven't they, taken a huge risk to make this tableau…" She pointed at the picture of the girl on the grave, and shrugged. "Just thinking aloud, but to me it seems like half a job. She's barefoot, no bouquet, do you see where I'm going with it?"

"Something else to bear in mind, Sue. Okay go home now, back in as early as you can make it tomorrow, let's get on with this, yeah?"

Chapter 18

Before she left, Tanya rang the mortuary. She intended to leave a message, a reminder that they had another girl at risk, but a woman answered. She confirmed Simon Hewitt was still there but point blank refused to let her speak to him.

"He's busy, he needs to get home. It's been a long day." The receptionist sounded cranky, tired. "We're all busy. Somebody will let you know as soon as he has something to tell you."

"Tonight?" Tanya asked.

"Probably not tonight. Have you any idea what it's like down here? I said, as soon as we have something."

"I'll send one of my team over there in the morning."

"You can do that if you want but it won't speed things up. I've already told you twice."

"Well, thanks for that." She slammed the phone back into the cradle. "Bitch."

She glanced up, Charlie was watching from the doorway, grinning. She laughed. "I know, it's not her fault and everybody's busy but there's Millie, isn't there?"

"Yeah. Look we've done all we can for now. There are people looking at the CCTV for the area, though to be honest, out in the sticks there isn't much. You've got the team sorted for tomorrow. We might as well go home."

"Yes. Go on, you go. I'll just finish up here." With a wave of his hand, he'd gone.

She went through it all again, stood in front of the boards, raised a hand to touch the picture of Sarah, nothing helped. She gathered up her things and left.

* * *

The house was quiet, calm, but she couldn't settle, there was a nagging pain behind her eyes and her shoulders were tense and tight. She tried some stretching exercises. It helped a bit. She made tea, poured it away after the first sip, made toast and ate it standing by the window peering out at the damp road. Thoughts whirled and replayed over and over. What she needed was a time-out. She needed to think about something else, clear her head.

She had been back in the house for just over a month now, waiting to be assigned, helping out in the Missing Persons division until this case had come up. It was her big chance and she couldn't screw it up. She wouldn't screw it up, but obsessing was unhealthy and pointless. She had done all that she could, now she had to wait for other people, frustrating as that was.

Upstairs she had arranged to have new wardrobes fitted around two walls of the spare room. Once her tenants had moved out she had brought in the decorator and joiner, planned just what she wanted to take it back, make it hers again, and she needed the storage space. She had started the job of sorting and moving her things before she had the call from Bob Scunthorpe to join the Operation Archer team and she had dropped everything to read about it, catch up before she met Charlie Lambert, but now it would be a mindless sort of task to get back to.

She looked at the boxes and the suitcases. There was too much, she knew she bought too much. It was so easy with the internet available twenty-four seven and she didn't try very hard to fight the temptation to shop. It was no-one else's business and she refused to feel guilty. She went in and flung open the doors, there were sensor lights, shelves, cupboards, drawers, all new and clean. It had cost an arm and a leg, but it had been worth it, it looked like something out of a magazine. She smiled.

After an hour sorting, re-hanging, and discarding, she was satisfied; calmed, and tired. There were three bags of things for the tip. She'd stick them in the boot of the car and chuck them when she had time. Her work clothes were separated from the leisure wear, colour co-ordinated, organised. Her bags and shoes in plastic covers. She was satisfied. The niggle of the case had been there in the background, but her headache had gone, she felt less wound up. A long hot shower washed away the grime and the tension and minutes after she climbed under the duvet she was asleep.

Chapter 19

"Amanita virosa."

"I'm sorry?" Simon Hewitt was on the phone. He had a smooth voice, calm and soft. It was pleasant listening to him after the harridan that had answered the call. It was the same woman as yesterday, short tempered and defensive, who had made her wait to be connected. Tanya had tutted and sucked her teeth.

"She's a bit of a bitch but she runs the place like clockwork." Charlie had told her. "She's not so bad once you get to know her and for heaven's sake don't get on the wrong side of her, you'll never get through to anyone."

Now that she had him on the line the pathologist seemed to be speaking a foreign language.

"Your poor lady. She died of poisoning. I was going to give you a call, thought I'd give you time to get organised."

Was that a complaint? Tanya glanced at her watch. Half past eight, the team were all in, everyone was working, so probably not; he was just being kind, considerate. She jotted down what she thought might be the correct spelling, or at least near enough to be able to Google it.

"Where do you get that then? Is it one of those designer drugs?"

He laughed, but she wasn't offended, it wasn't that sort of laugh. "No indeed. Far older than that and totally natural. The common name is Destroying Angel and it's a fungus."

"Fungus, like erm…" She couldn't think of an example that wasn't disgusting, she remembered adverts for treatment of nail fungus, bathroom mould, and anyway was that fungus?

He filled the silence, "Many people would say they were toadstools I suppose, but that's not strictly true. It's a common misconception that mushrooms are edible, and toadstools are not. Anyway, that's what poisoned this lady. They are very common, grow in deciduous and oak woodland pretty much all summer, they are rather sneaky in that they do look a little like what you might call a supermarket mushroom, the sort you have with your breakfast, but no, these little blighters are not so innocent. Not innocent at all. They account for a number of deaths from poisoning each year. You have to really know what you're about and far too many amateurs take to the woods with a nice little wicker basket which they happily load up with all sorts of problems. If you know what's what, there are quite specific differences of course."

"So, she could have eaten them by accident?"

"Well yes, she could have done, but that would be a little strange don't you think? She would have been ill about ten hours later, maybe a little more. Very ill. Stomach cramps, vomiting, diarrhoea, feeling very poorly. I doubt she would have been setting off on holiday, it doesn't really fit with your timeline. Unless her kidnapper took her while she was ill, held her somewhere even though she was in great distress; an odd scenario I would have thought. Of course, you will probably want to question her family, anyone who ate with her in the hours before her disappearance, but to be frank, assuming they had the same meal, they would be dead by now or at the very least extremely ill."

"Could she have been given them without her knowing?"

"It's possible yes, in a drink maybe, something with the right flavour, not coffee but maybe herbal tea, a stew, a soup, maybe even in a salad or sandwich. You don't need much, one cap is enough and if it was chopped small, well you wouldn't notice it in a mixture of other flavours. I suppose whoever took her must have fed her and then it was just too late. I don't know whether this will make you feel better or worse to be honest, but it would have made no difference when you found her."

"How do you mean?"

"Once she had ingested the poison she was, in effect, doomed."

"What if she had been given treatment though? If we'd found her sooner?"

"I'm afraid not. There is no antidote, there is no treatment. Once in a while, if the problem is diagnosed quickly and the patient's blood can be filtered through charcoal, the kidneys dialysed, maybe a liver transplant performed, and with a huge amount of luck, people have been saved but realistically, even these days, there is not much that can be done, recovery is a very, very long hard road and one would never be quite the same again."

"Would she have suffered, Doctor Hewitt?"

"Call me Simon, please. Yes, I'm very much afraid she would, it would have been extremely unpleasant for her. I'll send you my report but apart from that there isn't much more to say. Her stomach was empty, no chance of deciding just what she had eaten to get the poison into her system. There was evidence of vomiting and diarrhoea, kidney and liver damage in keeping with my other findings, just what was to be expected. Nothing under her nails, which had been damaged, maybe by clawing to escape from somewhere. They were cleaned and then painted afterwards, presumably when she was dead. The varnish wasn't chipped you see. As you surmised at the church she had been washed in bleach, her clothes, her hair everything. She hadn't been tied up, not abused sexually or beaten. She was a fit young woman, nothing unusual."

"Except she was dead?"

"Basically yes, except she was dead."

"I'll let you get on, Inspector. If you need anything else, please give me a call." He laughed, "If you can get past Moira."

Tanya turned to her screen, Googled the mushrooms, and decided after reading about them that she would never go picking mushrooms in the woods. She would even be a bit wary of the ones in the supermarket. She turned to Charlie. "God, Charlie, we're on the edge, all the bloody time."

He waited for more but there wasn't any. Tanya just turned back to her computer.

Chapter 20

"I've got an appointment with Bob Scunthorpe at half past ten." As Tanya pushed away from her desk, slurping the last of her coffee, Charlie glanced at his watch.

"Okay."

"Can you make sure everyone's bang up to date, working on the tasks, got the paperwork sorted, all that stuff? Just in case."

"Just in case?"

"Well, you know, just to make sure we're not missing anything. That there's nothing we should have done that we haven't. I don't want to leave any loose ends for him to tug at."

"I don't see what there could be."

"I suppose not but I just feel as though we're not moving very quickly, it seems stalled somehow. We haven't found where she was kept, why she was taken, why she was left where she was. We didn't save her, had no chance to really, and we still have Millie completely vanished."

"But, I don't see how anyone else could have done more than we did. We had nothing to go on, no ideas at all and then, she was only found yesterday. I did everything I should have done, before you came, when she was still just a missing person."

Tanya turned to look at him. "I wasn't criticising, Charlie, not for a minute, please know that. I just want to make sure this is watertight. I want to be certain there's nothing that they can pick at later when they look at what we've done." She turned without waiting for an answer and swung out of the office and down the corridor.

Charlie looked through the office window at the murder board in the other room. He couldn't think of anything more that they should have done but Tanya was right, it hadn't been enough.

* * *

Tanya liked Bob Scunthorpe, he'd helped her in the past when she'd been a Detective Constable working with a difficult inspector. He smiled when she came in, offered her a seat and a coffee. Tanya sat but refused the drink. He pulled a thin brown file towards him across his desk, flipped it open and then raised his eyes to look at her. "Unfortunate."

"Yes sir. Very sad. Not the outcome we would have hoped for."

"Quite. How are you coping with it?"

"Well, as I say, not what we would have hoped for. It was grim telling her boyfriend."

He nodded. "Never easy, good that you went yourself. Can you handle this, Tanya?"

"I've worked on five murders, sir. The last one was the woman in the river. The fingers cut off. We had a good result on that one, the case seems pretty sound, shouldn't be any problems when it comes to trial."

"Yes." He sighed. "Inspector Stanley's last case, we miss him. You were with him a fair bit I think. We were friends, Tony and I."

"Yes, he helped me prepare for my promotion, he taught me a lot, I felt as if I was learning from one of the best."

Bob smiled. It was a bit of flannel, but she had meant it.

"Sir, I'm going to solve this. She was only found yesterday. Until we get all the reports back there's not too much to go on, but I'll find whoever did this and I am going to work very hard to get Millie back safe and sound... They seem like a good team, I think they were a bit put out at first, understandably, but I don't see any major problems and Detective Inspector Lambert has been very professional. It must have stung, me coming in but he's been very supportive," Tanya said.

I suppose you could say, sir, that it's always been a murder," she continued.

"How's that?"

"As soon as she was given the poison, this Amanita virosa."

He glanced at the file, ran his finger down the page, and nodded.

"As soon as she was given that, it was a murder, she just wasn't dead yet." As she said it, it sounded awful to her ears. It was too late to take it back. She bit her tongue.

"Good point, nasty but true. Right." He flipped the file closed. "No problems with Kate?"

"No sir." Tanya shook her head.

"Good, she has had issues in the past. She isn't far from retirement, sometimes that makes it difficult for officers working with younger colleagues of a higher rank. It's good if she's settled with you."

Tanya made a mental note: *Keep an eye on Kate. Make sure she's happy.*

The Chief Inspector pushed the file aside. "I have faith in you Tanya, Tony always spoke highly of you." He noticed her smile, gave a small lift of his head in response. "Tanya, don't let pride get in the way. If you need help; if you find you're floundering, my door is open. There's no shame in requesting assistance. Okay?"

"Yes sir. Thank you, sir."

"Good luck."

Tanya nodded.

"I think that now you must make the missing woman a priority. Sarah Dickinson is dead, it's unfortunate but make Millie Roberts a priority. Let's see if we can save her."

"Sir."

She couldn't punch the air, she couldn't do a happy dance. There was a woman dead, a woman missing and two families grieving. Inside she couldn't hold down the fizz of excitement. She had the seal of approval. One more step along the road, it was just a small one, but significant. She had to get this right, for the victims of course, but for herself as well. She squared her shoulders, smiled at the secretary on the way out and strode down the corridor, her brain whirling with the next steps and the ones after that.

When she arrived back at the office Sue was standing in the doorway talking to Charlie, she blushed when Tanya tapped her on the shoulder.

"Right well, I'll get back to it, Charlie." She turned and walked back to her desk.

Charlie watched her go.

"Does she have a problem?" Tanya put her things on the desk and swivelled her chair to face him.

"No, it's fine."

"She seemed a bit awkward."

"Well, I guess she's just getting used to the idea. Both of us here and that. She was doing a fair bit of the leg work with me, before. I think maybe she's just a bit disappointed with what's happened."

"If she's got a problem, Charlie, tell her to come and talk to me, not sneak around behind my back, yeah?"

He nodded at her, "Okay boss."

It was the first time he'd called her that. She would tell him to call her Tanya but just this once, today, she grinned at him. "Come on we've got stuff to do. A murdering

bastard to find and a woman to rescue." As she said it she
felt the weight of reality. Was it already too late for Millie?

Chapter 21

The team were all there, the air smelled of coffee and toast. Everyone turned to where Tanya had taken up what was fast becoming her usual position beside the notice boards. She perched on the corner of the nearest desk. She told them about the discussion with the Chief Inspector, that they had his approval, that he was satisfied that they were doing everything they should. She was paraphrasing, sharing his confidence in her with them. It was the right thing to do, paying it forward. She was aware of the grins, a couple of nods. They were coming over to her side. Sue didn't look up, she was fiddling with the computer mouse.

"Right. Let's have a brainstorming session, shall we?" She turned to look at the white boards. "If you could make sure that any relevant information is added on here, that would be great. We need to record everything. So, how about you kick off, Sue," she said.

Sue stood up and opened her notebook, she glanced round, her eyes resting on Charlie who was looking at the notes in his hand – suddenly it was clear. Tanya felt a little fizz of sadness for the girl, she was young after all. But Charlie was married, he was a daddy and they were all professionals. She wondered if he realised.

Sue had begun to speak, "The dress. So, the shop that it came from – going by the name on the label – is part of a chain but it's been closed for a few years. They were nationwide at one stage, but they went out of business. It means we can't ask questions, chase payment or anything like that, I'm afraid, and it's not possible to get a very accurate time scale because there are hardly any references to them anywhere. I did think that I'd be able to find the style in a catalogue or something, get a year at least, but I'm not having a lot of luck."

She flicked through pages of printouts as she spoke, "There's absolutely no chance of even finding what area it was bought in, because the dresses were imported to order. Girls try on a model in the shop, all the shops carried almost all the models, and then a new one is made for them. I got this from Facebook, excited women giving out clues about style and what have you. It didn't lead very far. For most of them it was so long ago that they are already putting up baby scans and christening pictures. I suppose our dress must have been stored somewhere, but I guess people do that don't they? Keep them in cupboards for sentimental reasons and that."

"Do they?" Tanya glanced at Paul. "Is that right?"

"Yeah, well as I say my wife's is still in the family, so I guess they do. So, this bloke, I suppose we're assuming the person who abducted her, killed her, aren't we? Well, has to be." He looked around the room, there were a couple of nods in response. "Maybe it was his mother's, his sister's or of course his wife's. Though if she was still around, surely she'd notice. It's not a little thing, all that..." He couldn't find the word and they laughed as he wagged his hands in the area of his waist.

"Flounces," said Kate. "They call them flounces but yes you're right, it would fill your average Ikea wardrobe, you'd never get the door closed, so maybe a trunk or just in a plastic cover, in an attic."

Tanya spoke, "They'll be going over it with a fine-toothed comb in the lab, but with the bleach..." She shrugged. "Back to the question though. I think we have to assume it's the same person. Though there is no certainty that he hasn't got an accomplice, could it be a woman, and this is her dress? It's something else we should bear in mind. Thanks Paul."

Sue took over again, "As I say, because of the history with the shop, his bride, if there was a bride, could be long gone."

Kate raised a hand, "What does all this say about Millie, though? We have assumed that this was the same man, the events seemed to be the same. Woman alone, single man. We've shown his picture to our witness from the first time and she isn't sure but wouldn't rule it out either. But if he did it to poison Sarah and then dress her like this, does that mean he's got another dress? Why would he have two and if they cost thousands then does that mean he's wealthy?"

Charlie moved across the room, "Charity shops." A couple of the others murmured their agreement. Tanya shook her head, "How do you mean?"

"Charity shops sell wedding dresses."

"What? You mean, second hand?" She couldn't keep the appalled expression from her face. "People buy their wedding dresses second hand? No, surely not."

"Yeah. Not everyone keeps them. My wife didn't, she gave hers to a mate who was getting married later. But a lot of people give them to the charity shops for brides who can't afford to spend that sort of money."

Charlie grinned at the look on her face. "I've seen 'em, in the windows."

Sue spoke out, "So, maybe there never was a bride. Maybe he bought it specially."

Tanya shook her head, "Okay, so we need to start visiting these charity shops. I assume mostly it would be women buying wedding dresses, so perhaps a man, if he did buy it himself, would stick in somebody's memory. We've got a fair stretch of the motorway to cover and he might have bought it anywhere. Bigger towns first, it's going to take a while, I'll see if we can get help from some of the CIOs. It does at least give us something to work with. Well done everyone. Good thinking. If this guy has been buying wedding dresses, it could be the breakthrough. Find him, we find Millie."

She moved a little to the side, pointed to the picture on the second board. "Millie, we need to be concentrating on her disappearance. Sarah is important and tracing the dress, I should think, is vital but let's keep Millie as a priority. Where are we with her phone? I suppose it's too much to hope that they've been able to trace it."

Kate held up a hand, "It left the services and then they lost it. They reckon that probably it was tossed out onto the carriageway. They've asked the maintenance people, the traffic officers to be aware and they've been great – they sent a team to do the hard shoulder, but if it was thrown the other way, into the traffic there'd be nothing left of it in minutes. They'd have to close the motorway if we sent a team to look for it and frankly, there's just no point now."

Tanya stared for a long minute at the map of the road, the plan of the services where Millie had been. "Okay, Sue, before you go out can you go through the film from the traffic cameras? Find out where they lost the signal for the phone and take the time for about an hour after Millie and her friend were dropped off at the café. If the distance includes a junction, you'll have to do both carriageways. I'll be honest, I don't hold out much hope. This man seems camera aware, look at where he parked his car, the way he keeps his face averted. I expect that when he flung the phone he did it in the middle of heavy traffic, probably surrounded by trucks and what have you, but we have to do it. Get on to that now, will you?"

* * *

"Do you want coffee, Charlie?" They were back in the office, the clatter of the team gearing up to leave sounded good, it felt as though they were moving on.

With her mug in her hand, Tanya slid in behind her desk, closed her eyes. Her head was buzzing, she needed to still the clamour in her brain, needed a moment of calm, distance. "How's your wife?"

"Not too bad thanks. Some days she's stronger and doing stuff outside the house, something that's necessary. I think it helps. She's out with her sister today."

"That's good. You've got a big family."

"Yeah and getting bigger all the time." He smiled. "We have get togethers most weekends, Christmas and all that. Gets a bit noisy but I love it. Sorry I was rattling on there, but my family, we're all a bit close. Don't you ever try and keep in touch with yours? Did you say you've got a sister?"

"That's right. No we don't speak, not so much, the odd phone call. Nothing between us. It's nice, you and all your siblings and everything, but it's not for me. Too much room for disappointment, problems. I like my life simple."

Dan knocked on the open door. "We're all going out now." He held out a bunch of papers. "There's dozens of those charity shops. Kate printed them out, divvied them up into areas." Tanya reached out, took the sheets from his hand, and riffled through them.

He obviously had something else to say. He coughed. "That Steven Blakely is back on the internet. I made him a contact on Twitter when we started this. He's Tweeting again, I'm afraid we're not coming out of it very well."

"Damn." Tanya turned to her laptop, opened the account which she too had bookmarked. She read through some of the posts, the reposts and the responses. The police were coming in for quite a hammering, no names yet but maybe it was just a question of time. In a way, she couldn't blame him. He was hurting, and he had no-one to lash out at but them. She turned back to Dan. "Some of these shops are for Kate to visit?"

"Yep. They've got names on the tops of the pages."

"Right, Charlie and me, we'll take those." She glanced up, Charlie reached over to grab his jacket. "I'll catch you up. Let me just go and speak to Kate."

She caught the other woman just about to leave the hallway. "Kate, sorry but I need you to stay here. Steven Blakely is back on Twitter. I need someone to monitor his posts but more importantly, the responses. It could be that the killer will pick up on it, he might feel compelled to speak. Okay?" There was a flash of something across the other woman's face, disappointment, anger, it was hard to tell.

She nodded, turned back to the incident room and pulled off her coat. Tanya walked over to the desk, "If there's anything at all, let us know straight away, yes?" She needed to get a handle on this woman, the team were fitting together well, she didn't want any outsiders, it always caused trouble. "Thanks."

As she reached the door, Kate called across the room. "Can I have a word?"

"Of course."

"Do you know how old I am?"

"Not exactly, no."

"Okay, well, I'm fifty." As Tanya opened her mouth to speak, the other woman held up her hand.

"Don't please. I know I look my age. It's fine, I've never been vain. But, I run three times a week, I swim nearly every night and I have done two triathlons this year and have another one in about six weeks."

"Wow." Tanya was genuinely impressed. "Well, I thought I was fit but, blimey."

"The thing is though." There was a pause, Kate looked down at her hands. "Don't treat me as if I'm past it. I know I'm the oldest, I know my career is stalled. I'm not going any higher but that's okay as well because I've raised three kids, got a good marriage. I'm happy with the stuff I've done. But, you know, don't write me off."

"I haven't, I wouldn't do that." Tanya had turned back into the room, held out a hand, let it drop again.

"It's just that, calling me back, asking me to stay behind instead of going out on the road, it feels a bit as though I'm being side-lined. It's the second time, Charlie did it as well, I don't want to just be the one in the office, you know."

"Right. Right. I see. Okay, the reason I've done this, and honestly Kate I wouldn't lie to you, Dave had just handed me a bunch of papers, collated and organised, dividing up the charity shops into areas and allocating bodies. I was impressed. He told me you'd done it. The monitoring of Steven Blakely's tweets needs somebody on the ball, somebody who might be able to pick up on anything relevant. I thought of you. I've been impressed with your work on the computer, your organisational skills. I want to catch this bastard, I want to save this other girl. To do that I need to utilize everyone's particular talents. It might seem less 'sharp end' than being out on the road, I grant you that, but it's the best thing for the case, nothing more." She had meant every word and the smile creeping across Kate's face told her she'd got it right.

Tanya stopped as she turned to the door. "Are we okay Kate?"

Kate nodded. "Yes boss. Thanks."

Chapter 22

It was a long day for all of them. They trawled dozens of charity shops. At the end of it Tanya felt grubby and depressed. As she had expected there had been no image of a phone flung from a car window, though there was plenty of other detritus hurled from the passing traffic. Sue had gone over and over it, and managed to get some help from the civilian investigators. She had zoomed in on every likely looking incident, recorded dozens of events. The maintenance crews had found nothing, and Tanya didn't see any value in spending more time trying to trace a phone which would, even if it hadn't gone under the wheels of a juggernaut, be shattered plastic and very little more.

They didn't meet back in the office, Tanya had kept in touch with the rest of the team by phone and text and they scheduled a Skype conference for evening.

She had a long, long shower. Wrapped in her towelling bath robe she strolled into the guest room, newly converted into her dressing room. She didn't feel guilt, she had worked for this. It was her money after all, but she did feel sad, sad that for some people, some women, finding her cast offs, the things that she had fished from the car boot and left at the Cancer Research shop, finding her throwaways would be thrilling.

It had all come back, the limp washed up feel of old skirts and dresses, faded by time. The school blouses with frayed cuffs, jeans with ragged hems, and then, the blazer stained by her sister's leaking fountain pen. That had been the final straw. She was going into a new school, new friends, it was supposed to be a new start. She had cut at it with scissors, thrown the jacket into a skip outside one of the local houses and refused to even discuss the school until she was promised a new uniform. There had been tears and recriminations, it had been a turning point.

She knew she had been a mistake. The second daughter too soon after the first. She never had anything new, just for herself. It had hurt when she learned to understand. The older she had become the more it had hurt. She was left in no doubt that she had been an unwanted child and felt she had never really caught up, always referred to as Fiona's sister, always compared to her brilliant sibling and found wanting.

Until, that is, she finished her degree and joined the police force. On the day of the passing out parade, at last, she had seen the shine of pride in her mother's eyes that she had looked for all her life. It had come late, her father was gone and her mother already ill and to be dead within the year, but at least they had come to an understanding before the end and Tanya didn't hold a grudge. However, she had vowed that the things she had, the clothes she wore, would be the best that she could buy. She'd worked hard, studied hard, she deserved her stuff, but tonight she didn't open the wardrobe doors, didn't feel quite right looking at clothes that she hadn't even properly unpacked yet. The volunteers, the customers, the endless racks of second hand belongings had depressed her, brought back feelings that had long buried.

She went down to the kitchen, poured wine, cooked savoury rice, tried to concentrate on the missing girls, going over what they knew as fact. This wasn't a time to start thinking about fairness, there was nothing fair about what happened to Sarah Dickinson, what might be happening right now to Millie Roberts. Things were just things, but it was life, opportunity, that was irreplaceable.

* * *

The team compared notes, swapped information on the Skype video but at the end of the day it was worrying and disappointing how little they had really accomplished. Paul had been to one shop that told him they sold wedding dresses, bridesmaids outfits, cocktail gowns to the local amateur dramatics groups and so, yes, sometimes men would come in and buy those things. Dan told them that one of the places he visited had a regular contingent of transgender customers and a whole section they kept for fancy dress outfits that included wedding dresses. Generally, they were the ones with thigh high slits or low-cut backs, revealing bodices, but again both men and women bought them.

It was obvious from the mood of the chat they were all feeling down, what they had thought would be a good lead turned out to be so much less.

She needed to gee them up a bit, "Okay. At least we have more information. It's not going to be as easy as we thought, but we know it's a possibility, a probability, he bought the dress second hand. We'll regroup tomorrow, can we all manage seven thirty?" They agreed. "Thanks for this today, it feels like a bit of a let-down just now but it's all useful information and it's more than we had before."

Sue spoke up just before they all shut down. "Has Kate had any luck with the Twitter stuff?"

"No, she's been monitoring Steven Blakely's Facebook page, and the memorial page they have set up for Sarah. There's plenty of activity apparently but nothing that has jumped out at her. A lot of the usual sentimental outpouring. I am going to go through some of it myself now, just to help out."

"Do you want us to do some as well?" Dan said.

"No, there's no need and we can go over the print outs tomorrow anyway, thanks though. You guys get some rest and we'll get back to it in the morning. Good night."

She shut off Skype and dropped her head into her hands. It was a disappointment, more than she had let on, but their luck had to change sometime. It just had to.

She rang Charlie. As he answered the phone she realised that she didn't know what he could say that hadn't already been said. She had just, quite suddenly, felt alone, a little overwhelmed by the responsibility and it was an odd feeling for her, unexpected and unsettling. "Sorry Charlie, I hate disturbing you at home. I just needed someone to talk to."

"Do you want me to come over to you?"

"God no, I just, well to be honest I don't know why I called. We've said all there is to say. I'm frustrated I think, and impatient."

"Tanya, you need to get some sleep. You're tired, we all are. You'll be fine tomorrow. Really you will. You've got this."

She could hear the baby crying in the background and felt guilty and feeble, needy.

"Yeah, sorry Charlie."

"See you tomorrow. Get some sleep."

She turned back to her laptop, clicked on the page she had bookmarked two days ago. They were nice boots, good expensive boots. She pressed buy.

* * *

She had three hours of restless snoozing, waking over and over with the thoughts and ideas spinning in her head. She tried to relax, tried to clear her mind but nothing worked and when the mobile phone on her bedside table lit and began to vibrate she snatched it up with a feeling of relief, even though she knew that a call in the early hours of the morning couldn't be good news.

"Miller." She snapped on the light. Before the dispatcher at the other end of the line had finished speaking she was already sliding out of bed and pulling clothes from her underwear drawer.

Chapter 23

This church was more imposing than the last one, bigger, more affluent looking. It was another pretty building, the nave extending impressively from the foot of its square tower. There was a small porch, great dark wood doors, and a little apex roof, shining wet in the growing light, fancy windows, ancient trees.

It had taken just half an hour to drive through the deserted country roads from Oxford. As she crossed the motorway, Tanya glanced from the bridge, the carriageways were not empty, never, but they were quiet at this early hour.

As she pulled onto the verge at the side of the road she noticed lights in upstairs windows nearby, and saw the flutter of a curtain as someone peered out at the early morning disturbance. Already there were patrol cars, an ambulance parked beside the entrance to a small row of lock up garages, the blue light thrown back by the pale stone walls of the church. For a moment hope flared, an ambulance wouldn't be called for a dead body, but then the black van from the mortuary pulled around the corner in front of her, drawing to a halt just beyond the churchyard entrance.

Tanya showed her warrant card to the young constable at the gate, and pointed to the small group clustered near the ambulance. "What's that about?"

"Poor bugger who called it in. Thought he'd seen a ghost, fell off his bike. They reckon he's broken his arm, but right now they're trying to calm him down a bit. He's in a shocking state."

She crossed the damp grass. There was a policewoman, standing with her arm around the shoulders of the old man just inside the back door of the ambulance, she nodded at Tanya.

"This is Mr Morris, they need to get him to hospital but we've been sorting him out a bit first." She indicated the sling on his arm. Tanya leaned close to the patient who was shuddering and shaking under the silver blanket.

"Mr Morris, I know this has been horrible for you, but I wonder if you can just give me a quick idea about this morning?"

He shook his head. "Scared me bloody stupid it did. I come down here every day, every day, never had nothing like this happen."

"It's early, are you always out and about this early?"

"Aye. I'm a baker, going in to light my ovens, I always come down this way. On my bike see, no cars normally, nice and quiet. Don't know that I'll ever do it again after this."

"Can you describe what happened?"

He pulled the blanket tighter to his throat, shuddered again. "Well, I suppose nothing really happened, not as such. I was just pedalling down beside the graveyard, never bothered me that, not till now anyway. I glanced over and…" He shook his head. "I can't tell you, I just can't. never believed in ghosts, all that nonsense, but when I saw that. Well." He pointed to his knees where the trousers were torn, blood seeping through the fabric. "I lost control, went arse over elbow, landed slap in the middle of the road. I were terrified, truly, thought I was gonna have a heart attack. Anyway, I dragged meself up, and then I saw what it was, that thing. I thought it might be a dummy, you know, like one of the fake ones they have in shop windows, but I wasn't going in there, wasn't getting near, so I just dialled 999. It's a woman, isn't it? Some poor bloody woman. Who'd do a thing like that, eh?"

"I don't know, Mr Morris, but I'm doing everything I can to find out." She nodded to the paramedic and moved away, watching as they helped him further into the vehicle.

The sky was streaked now with pink, the trees gaining colour in the growing dawn. They hadn't erected the plastic cover yet and sequins and silver threads caught the light, glittering like pink fireflies as the breeze stirred the filmy fabric of the gown. It was beautiful and terrible. Long blond hair shifted and swayed, the ends flicking over a pale face.

"Detective Inspector." At the sound of his voice she turned to see Simon Hewitt striding towards her, pulling up the hood of his paper suit, tucking in his dark hair. He leaned to shake her hand. "I'm sorry to see you again in such circumstances."

She nodded, watched as he pulled up the mask, noted that there was no ring on his finger as he pushed it into the blue gloves.

Well that didn't mean anything, nothing at all.

"Looks like something similar to the last one," she murmured.

He nodded, "Well, we'll see, won't we. From what I've been told there are obvious similarities but as soon as I have any solid information I'll let you know."

She knew, she knew already that this had to be Millie. It was going to be a long hard day, there were going to be some difficult conversations. "I'd appreciate anything you can tell me as soon as it's possible." Hewitt nodded at her and then strode on towards the tragic figure, stroked now with growing light from the rising sun, beads and baubles glinting prettily.

* * *

By the time she reached the office, Charlie was already there, already making coffee. "The team are on the way in." He held out a cup, offered her the bag of pastries. In spite of the scene she had just left, Tanya was hungry. She pulled out a chocolatine, dipped it into her cup and groaned with pleasure as she pushed the sweet, chocolaty mush into her mouth.

Chapter 24

Toast and coffee again. Tanya wondered if the homely smell would always remind her of these days, these dead women. She wondered who it was bringing their breakfast up from the canteen but couldn't ask; hadn't she and Charlie done exactly the same thing, albeit from the shops outside? But there was something about the old-fashioned smell of toast, it was the smell of home that seemed wrong in this room where the pictures of Millie's dead body in her silver dress had joined the ones of her grinning and smiling on holiday just a few days ago.

She perched on the desk, the team found their places, settled down. "Right, well I don't think there can be very much doubt that this is the same as Sarah. We are waiting for the pathologist of course, but I'm going to be very surprised if it's not the same method. There was no blood visible, no damage to the body that I could see from where I stood. This dress is simpler. A bit medieval I suppose, with those long, flowing sleeves, the high waist, but I'm not sure that's relevant, though of course we should keep an open mind. It looks like a wedding dress to me, so please email an image to your contacts at the charity shops from yesterday to see if any of them remember it. It's lovely isn't it? Now there is one thing that is different, and I wasn't able to see it at first from my position, not until we received the pictures, but look at her hair." Tanya pointed to the close up.

"Tinsel," said Sue, "The tinsel is round her head."

Tanya nodded. "It would make sense then, that the piece that we found last time," she held up the evidence bag, "was round Sarah's head. It looks long enough anyway."

There was silence for a moment. Paul spoke out, "Maybe he was making her into a queen, with a crown, you know."

Tanya nodded, scribbled on the board.

From his place in the back of the room Dan Price coughed, they turned to him.

"Nativity," Dan said in a low voice. He blushed now he had the attention of the whole room, but he stood up, and pointed towards the noticeboard.

Tanya tipped her head to one side, "Sorry?"

"My kid sister, she's a lot younger than me. Still at school and I went to the Christmas concert last year. They did a nativity, there was a bit of a fuss about it, they had it sort of multi-faith in the end, but with the baby and shepherds, that stuff." He waved his hand in the air dismissively. He was bright red by now, couldn't meet anyone's eyes.

"Yes," Charlie stepped in. "So, they used tinsel? What for, trimming?"

"Yeah, some for that, but the little girls, they wore it on their heads."

Sue interrupted and rescued him. "Angels?"

He breathed a sigh of relief, nodded. "Yeah. The angels had tinsel round their heads, like halos."

Tanya spoke slowly, turning to peer more closely at the photographs, "So, maybe she's not a bride then? With that on her head, it's a whatchamacallit – a halo."

"Yes, boss. I reckon so."

"Well done, Dan." She had meant to encourage him and all she did was cause him to blush an even deeper shade. He'd have to get over that, find some confidence; she smiled at him, nodded. "So, she, they, were angels." She hadn't meant to plunge them back into gloom, but she saw them, saw them read her thoughts, not *were angels*, not *were*. *Are*. If you believe in that stuff and some people still do.

"Hang on a minute." This from Kate who had turned to her desk, was scrolling through the screen on her computer, typing impatiently while she muttered under her breath. "There, yes. Hold on while I transfer it. They all turned to watch as the mirror of Kate's screen opened on the big monitor beside the boards. It showed a Twitter feed, they watched as she scrolled through the expressions of sympathy, the sickly-sweet comments, the thumbnails of laughing girls in bars, arms around each other, groups which would never again include Sarah. Kate stilled the image. "There, look!"

Tanya read the tweet aloud. "Don't grieve now, she is an angel."

The picture on the screen moved again, "And again here. I didn't take a lot of notice, there was so much stuff like this. She's at peace and what not, but here again, the same person. After Steven Blakely acknowledges the tweet with just a thank you." She enlarged the image so that they could all read it. "She has been spared to sit in beauty with the angels."

"Right." Tanya walked to Kate's desk, looked down at the smaller screen as if somehow it made it all more real. "Kate, get on to the IT department. We need to know where this was sent from, who the hell this is. Excellent, well done."

She was rewarded with just a short nod from the older woman but could see the pride in the set of her shoulders the way she slid into her desk chair, picked up the phone. "Charlie, take Dan, go and see, Steven, we need to tell him about this personally anyway, but see if he knows who this is, tweeting. I have to go and talk to Mr and Mrs Roberts."

The mood in the room had lifted, they could all feel it, this was something real, something positive.

Then Tanya's phone rang. The chatter quieted, a couple of them turned to look at her. Because, sometimes you just know.

Chapter 25

It wasn't bloody fair, it just wasn't. Why did they think it was alright to treat her like a sodding ping pong ball? Just because her stupid mother and loser dad couldn't keep their shit together, couldn't stay married, why did they think she had to be the one treated like a lump of bloody luggage, shuffled back and forth?

Jane was livid. Not only had her loser dad's new wife been there all bloody week, pawing and leering at him, which she thought was disgusting, then she'd had to share the bedroom with her dad's stupid, grotesque little step kid. Then he'd dropped her off here early to wait while they all went off to some feeble birthday party. Now she had to spend the weekend with her mother, and all of next week. Getting herself ready for school because mum's precious, bloody boss needed her in at eight in the morning; making her own tea, because he needed her to stay late. Well that was okay because all she had to do was stick some plates in the dishwasher and she could say she'd eaten.

She looked down at the chips in front of her, the burger in its paper wrapper. She wasn't eating this. Did he think she was like six or something? God, couldn't he see how fat she was already, she reached a hand to her waist, pinched at her skin. She was huge, fat and ugly and dumped in these scuzzy services waiting for her bloody mother who couldn't even get there on time. Why couldn't they just let her choose who she lived with, permanently, why couldn't they just let her decide? It was her bloody life.

She'd go. That's what she'd do. If they couldn't be bothered with her, she'd go. She grinned across at a couple of soldiers sitting a few tables away, the cute one with the shaved head winked at her.

She picked at the cooling chips, pushed the plastic plate away. That was so environmentally disgusting, plastic. Nobody cared. Bloody old people, they'd already ruined the world and there'd be nothing left by the time she left school, got a job, her own place, her own life.

She bent to pick up her backpack. She wasn't waiting any longer. If her stupid mother couldn't get there in time, then sod her. She'd go and blag a lift, get a ride and then she'd ring her from home. That'd show her, maybe then they'd stop treating her like a little kid. She sniffed, wiped away the tears of anger and frustration.

She saw his boots, his jeans, raised her head. She didn't speak, he was really old.

"Good evening young lady. Are you on your own?"

She didn't answer, she glared at him, opened her eyes wide, blew out a huff, turned away and pulled out her phone. That was when he flicked open the wallet and she saw the police badge, his picture. *Shit.*

"Are you on your own?"

"I'm waiting for my mum. She's been delayed. I'm fine."

"It's not safe for you to be here, have you not seen the notices?"

She hadn't, not really. She'd seen some stupid pictures, two women, she hadn't read them, they were nothing to do with her.

"We're concerned about young women on their own here and at the other service areas. We're especially worried about women looking like yourself." He pulled one of the posters from his pocket, held it out to her. Okay she could see, they both had hair like hers, blue eyes, they were sort of pretty, but they were ancient. She didn't look like them, not at all.

She needed him to go, this was well embarrassing, "I'm fine. Thank you."

"How long will it be before your mother arrives?"

"Well I don't know, do I? Stupid bitch, she's probably lost or something. Look I'll ring her, okay."

"I don't think you should use that attitude with me. I could arrest you, for your own safety, you know that, don't you?"

He couldn't, could he? That was bollocks, wasn't it?

"I'm sorry. Look not TBR or anything, but it's just been a long day, okay?"

"Tell you what, why don't you come and wait with me? I've got some coffee in the car, decent stuff not like they serve here."

Shit, she didn't want to be seen with this old man, he was rank, people might think he was her dad or something. Police should look smarter than this, police should wear proper uniforms. She glanced at the soldiers again, yeah uniforms are cool. She shook her head. "I don't drink coffee, it's crap."

He laughed, just a snort really, "Well okay, I've got herbal tea, water, don't suppose you drink that either?"

"Sometimes. But, look, okay, my mum'll be here soon. Honest, I'll just wait here."

"You okay here?"

OMG, it was the soldier, the one with the shaved head, *Oh my actual God, he's so hot.*

She was going to tell him, let him know that it was all fine, that she was in control and then, the stupid old bloke flashed his i.d. The soldier backed off, gave her a weird look. Great, now he thought she was some sort of scummer or something. Well, bloody typical.

"See, that's what I mean. You shouldn't be here on your own. Not at the moment, not looking like…" He stopped. "Tell you what, why don't you come and sit in my van? You can call your mum, and when she arrives she can pick you up outside. I'll make sure you're okay. Make sure you're safe."

She still didn't know if it was a good decision, but it was better than sitting in the café arguing and when her mum turned up she'd tell her the police had taken her in for protection and that would freak her out. Yeah.

The van was old, but it was blue, and it had a sort of badge on the side. Jane looked around, there were not many people about, not in this quiet corner beside the motel. She wasn't sure. She felt tears welling up again, her throat closing over.

She didn't feel right about this. "I think I'd rather just wait inside."

His hands were strong, hard, he had her around the arms, he was pushing her forward, forcing her inside. She tripped and fell across the floor. He pushed her legs in, grabbed at her backpack. Before she could recover, the sliding door slammed, and he was in the front seat. The engine was starting. She began to scream. She shuffled and scrabbled between the seats, pushed to her knees, but it was cramped and awkward.

"It's okay, don't be afraid. There's no need to be afraid, I'm going to look after you. You'll be alright." He was glancing round, shouting to her.

"Let me go. Let me go, please, please, please. God, don't do this. Please."

Now the van was moving, faster, faster, backing from the quiet, far corner of the car park, turning towards the motel. She tried to slide onto the seat. There wasn't room to scramble up. The van swerved, rocked. She tried to reach the window. His hand came back between the seats, he grabbed at her. She squirmed away. "Please don't, please. I'm sorry." She didn't know what she was sorry for, but as he roared away down the service road, and out into the fields at the back of Cherwell Valley she felt the cold draught from the window. His hand pulled back, she watched as the phone which he had pulled from the pocket in the front of her bag, flew out into the trees.

She was just so very sorry for everything.

Chapter 26

"Okay, change of plan. Charlie, come with me. Dan and Sue, will you talk to Steven Blakely? We've got a young girl missing at Cherwell Valley. The mother's in a state because her daughter is blond, blue eyed and slim. She's a lot younger than Sarah and Millie, just sixteen, but apparently looks older. Charlie and I will head down there now, see what's what. We'll let you know as soon as we get a clearer picture. Kate – I'm sorry Kate but could you visit the Roberts', they have a FLO with them. Have you done this before?" She was relieved to see the nod from Kate. She'd do it well, she knew what it was like to have children, must have thought about this situation whenever they were late home or not where they were supposed to be. It was a rotten job and she had been dreading it. If this other thing wasn't just so much worse, she could have felt grateful to be passing it on.

For a while Tanya was silent in the car, Charlie drove, she made notes on her tablet, opened folders to look at what they'd had before. "Shit Charlie, if this is another one I'm going to lose this, aren't I? Three women, Bob's not going to let me handle it, they'll hand it over to the Major

Crime Unit, I'd half expected it already. Bugger, bugger, I really don't want to screw this up."

He didn't answer, let her vent. He knew exactly how she felt but this wasn't the time to remind her of that.

She took a breath, closed her eyes for a minute and then spoke again, calmer now, regaining control. "Okay, we don't know for certain this is him again but, well yes, there is a strong possibility. Hold on." She took out her phone, flicked through the contacts until she found the mortuary number.

"Moira, it's Detective Inspector Miller. Simon said that I could give him a call if I needed help." She was stretching the truth, crossing her fingers.

"He's busy, he's doing a post mortem on your latest victim."

How did this woman manage to make it sound as if it was Tanya's fault? How did she do that?

She struggled, but kept the tone friendly, "Great, is there any chance you could ask him a question for me?"

"What is it?"

"I just need to know whether or not he has been able to decide if the cause of death is the same. It's really important, Moira. I might have another woman missing. I'd be really grateful."

"Hold on."

She shouldn't need to do this, she should just be able to ring up, ask the question and get an answer. Was it always going to be like this, finessing people, buttering them up? She sighed.

"Hello, Detective Inspector, I have Dr Hewitt for you."

"Detective Inspector Miller. Hello there. I was just about to give you a call, that's twice now, you must be reading my mind."

"I'm sorry to bother you. It's a quick question, Simon. Was Millie killed in the same way as Sarah?"

There was a pause, the shuffle of papers before he spoke again. "I have to wait for the results from the lab before I put it in writing but I'm assuming your need to know is urgent. So, I will stick my neck out and say that from what we have seen, yes. There is evidence of kidney and liver damage, there has been vomiting, the poor woman's throat was burned by acid, her bowels were empty, she was dehydrated. Yes, I would say this is the same, I will confirm later of course. Does that help?"

"I'm not sure that's the right expression. It may be that we've got another woman missing. If that's true and he's already been able to get her to eat or drink something containing the mushrooms how long have we got, before it's too late?"

"I'm really sorry to hear that. Probably about ten hours, maybe a short while longer, before she seems ill. She may appear to recover after that, but the damage will already have been done. Unless you find her immediately, administer an emetic and get her some treatment, then there is very little that anyone will be able to do. Just another note, Ms Roberts had been washed with bleach, as had the other victim, the dress had been thoroughly cleaned. I don't think there will be anything from that, though of course they are trying in the lab. Maybe, if, as I understand it, the killer is masquerading as a member of the force, well, I just wonder if it's possible he genuinely is, given the care he has taken to hide any physical traces. Not trying to teach you your job, Detective Inspector – Tanya – just throwing an idea in."

She thanked him and turned off the phone.

It was hopeless, wasn't it? If he had done the same as before this girl was already beyond their help. She should have done more to get the word out, should have made more fuss; damn it, she should have been able to stop this. Now she had to face this girl's mother and tell her not to worry, that they were doing everything they could. Simon had raised a good point as well. It had been in the back of her mind all along and now it must be faced. Had she been too keen to dismiss the idea that it was one of them, a colleague? Maybe the badge was genuine after all.

She hadn't been open enough to the idea, she could have done more, circulated what they had to the other forces, someone might have recognised him, someone who knew him well enough to see from his build or his stance. Maybe they could have flushed him out. They had closed ranks quickly, dismissed the idea almost out of hand. They had been wrong. On top of that, the confirmation that it was the same MO, logically the same killer, meant that surely she was going to be taken off the case. A serial killer, they would bring in the big guns of the Major Crime Unit, unless she could prove she was on the brink of solving it, and in truth she didn't think she was.

She thumped at the dashboard, it was a pointless thing to do and it didn't help. Charlie drove on in silence. Fear threatened to overwhelm her, she had to stop that, she had to remain detached, professional. She began to make notes, plan for the worst. She tried to hope for the best but deep inside she could feel it, this was him again. This was the reason for the fixed expression on Charlie's face, his fierce grip on the steering wheel. They both knew. She gave him a quick precis of the phone call. He didn't turn to look at her, he nodded – just once.

* * *

Patrol cars in front of the café, little groups of people trying not to stare, failing. The posters on the door as they went through the foyer, Sarah, Millie, both dead, it was awful. They climbed the stairs to the nasty little office where a different, younger man than the one she had been expecting, sat beside the sobbing woman. His badge identified him as an assistant manager. Tanya turned to Charlie and mouthed the word 'George'. He turned away, dialling the mobile number for Simpson, the manager they had met before.

The woman was beyond distraught. Between pleading that her daughter be found immediately with every available officer involved, she spent time cursing her ex-husband and his decision to 'abandon', her word, their only daughter just so that he could go off with his new family. She cried, raged, and begged and Tanya was so sorry for her. She knew though, that to do her job she must step back. Acknowledge the desperation, the anguish and then use that to spur her on. She made all the right noises. Arranged for a family liaison officer to be assigned. *How many more times am I going to have to do this?* She asked for pictures, looked at the image of the pretty young girl used as the wallpaper on her mum's phone and saw the similarities. Shining blond hair, slender build, pale skin.

Another angel.

As Charlie reached a hand towards the door it opened in front of him. The man standing outside in the hallway leaned round to peer into the room.

"George? Is he here? The manager?" He ignored the group clustered around Millie's mother and addressed the assistant manager directly. "I'm looking for George."

"Not just now, Peter," the younger man said.

"But I need to speak to him, we've got business to discuss."

Tanya glanced from one man to the other, saw Charlie disappear into the hallway. She spoke to the assistant manager, "Who's this?"

"A friend of George. Sorry, I'll get rid of him." He took the few steps across the small office and laid a hand on the intruder's shoulder. "Come on, Peter, we've got a bit of a situation here. George isn't in at the moment. I'll tell him you came."

"Right, thanks then. He'll know what it's about."

As he came back to the desk he apologised again. "George gives him stuff to do now and then, on a casual basis I think. He knows him personally."

"Okay. So, he's not actually employed here then?"

"No, not officially, as I say it's a personal arrangement between him and George, I don't get involved. George does stuff with charities, things like that, but it's nothing to do with the company."

Tanya made a note, they'd ask George about his extracurricular activities although they had to find him first.

Chapter 27

Once they had handed the stricken woman to a uniformed officer and arranged help to get her home, Tanya stepped out of the office to where Charlie stood watching through a narrow window. He was looking down on a scene that was so ordinary, so everyday, it didn't seem possible that this was happening. Yes, there were uniforms, more than usual, but there were children, teams in track suits and trainers, old guys in motor bike leathers looking faintly ridiculous and then dozens of ordinary people, couples, families, groups, and the women, on their own, living their lives, and it was them who needed her to fix this. They assumed it was safe, she had to make sure it was.

If only she could work out how.

"So, George Simpson?"

Charlie just shook his head. "No answer."

They walked around the services, looked at the table where Jane had been picked up on the CCTV, her head bent over the plate of food, untouched in front of her. She had looked like any ordinary teenager, a little angry, a little insecure. They had seen him, watched as he approached the table with his head turned away from the surveillance cameras. He had shown her the wallet and then she had, inexplicably, collected her belongings and walked out with him.

It was imperative to find the soldier who had approached her, as soon as possible. She had them send the video by email to the office and called to tell Paul to drop anything else he was doing and identify the badges, getting anyone else available to help. She instructed him find out who the hell this was, where he was, and to arrange to have him interviewed as soon as possible.

The soldier had looked at the killer in the face, he was priceless as a witness.

They watched as the two figures crossed the car park and vanished out of sight in the narrow road beside the hotel.

"Why would she do that? Why would anyone go and get in a car with a stranger, Charlie?"

"Well I guess it's because he's not really a stranger. As far as she knows he's a copper, he's safe."

They started across the car park, it was windy with rain in the air, late afternoon; the services were busy with a wide mix of people.

Tanya glanced around, laid a hand on Charlie's arm, and pointed into the parked cars. "What's going on over there?"

He turned to see a young woman, long blond hair blowing in the light breeze, attempting to pull her car door closed. A man in uniform was bending towards her, standing in a position that forced her to keep it open. She was obviously distressed, waving her arms at him. They couldn't make out the words but her voice, high pitched and angry, carried to them across the tarmacked space. They knew that it was ludicrous to think it could be anything to do with their case, it just didn't happen like that, but they couldn't walk away.

Pulling their i.d. from their pockets they approached the white Fiesta. The young woman, barely more than a girl, was crying. Charlie spoke, "Alright mate, can we help?" Although his uniform was official, and most members of the public wouldn't think about the difference, they had seen immediately that he wasn't a member of the police force. The man turned on them, held a hand up dismissively.

"It's fine thank you. I've got this."

Charlie moved closer, pushed his warrant card nearer to the man's face, forced him to look at it. "Would you mind telling us what's going on?"

The woman had, by this time stopped crying and was beginning to rant, "Bloody fascist!" Tanya held up a hand, shook her head.

"Right well, this lady was speeding. I followed her from the carriageway into the services and I am now having a word with her about her driving. I suggested she come and sit in our vehicle or inside the facility as it's raining, she refused."

"Bloody hell I was not speeding. I bloody wasn't."

Charlie pulled himself up to his full height, at more than six feet with broad shoulders, he was imposing even without a uniform. He looked down his nose at the traffic officer, "Did the traffic cameras pick this up?"

Less officious now, the shorter man answered, "I assume so."

The young woman still could not keep silent, "Nothing to bloody pick up was there. I didn't do nothing." Tanya put a finger to her lips, shook her head.

"Look mate, we've got a situation here." Charlie had pulled his copy of the poster from his jacket pocket. The motorway officer glanced at it.

"Yeah, I've seen that. Nothing to do with me."

"Well, I guess it is. It's something that we should all be aware of, should all be trying to help with, yes?"

There was no answer.

"Tell you what, the cameras will have picked it all up. If there has been an offence, then it'll be dealt with. Shall we all just move along?"

It was too much for the frustrated and embarrassed traffic officer, he turned ready to stride away. Charlie stopped him. "If I could just take your name, mate?"

"No, you bloody can't. I'm just doing my job here, trying to." He paused, knew that he didn't actually have a choice, and impatiently handed over his identification for Charlie to make a note. They watched as he clambered into his huge four-wheel drive and turned away towards the road.

Tanya had already begun asking the female driver for details, but it seemed that, apart from her fury at being stopped, and the continuous denial of any wrong doing, the girl was no longer particularly distressed.

What was of more concern was that, though she used the motorway daily, and the service areas often, she was unaware of the disappearance of Sarah and Millie. She hadn't read the notices, hadn't registered the warnings. They went through the motions, asking her if she'd been aware of any suspicious activity but they knew by now that it was going to lead nowhere.

They headed to the office, most of the drive was in silence, Tanya went over and over the scenes in her head. Looking for something, anything that she had missed. Once they were back Tanya rang to make an appointment with Bob Scunthorpe. It was only a question of time before he called her and surely it would look better if she made the first move.

She couldn't decide whether it was good or bad that he was available to see her immediately.

She stopped in the incident room on the way. "Run a check on that traffic officer will you, Charlie. Probably a waste of time but you never know."

"Already on it, boss."

Chapter 28

The Chief Inspector offered her coffee, she refused. "This is bad news, Tanya."

"Yes sir."

"So, what do you see as your next move?"

It was imperative that she let him know she was in control. She was at a point where there was nothing else to do but to plough on, and he had to believe it was all okay. "I think we have to have a two-pronged attack, sir." He raised his eyebrows.

Don't overcook it.

"We have to try and find this young woman as quickly as possible, obviously. We have an opportunity with a witness, a soldier. I've got the team on that now. We are trying to talk to the manager of the services who seems to have taken time off. Charlie and I both had a feeling that there was something off about him, and he has been known to us in the past."

Bob nodded, made a note.

She knew what she would say next was a thorny subject but after the incident in the car park, she saw that it had become unavoidable. She swallowed hard as he looked up at her.

"I need to take more steps to protect the public, sir. We need, as a matter of urgency, to alert people. We've got the notices but it's not enough. It's not doing the job." She gave him a brief account of the incident with the traffic officer. "That driver simply hadn't registered the situation, neither, it seems, had the motorway patrol bloke, although we are looking into him more closely, just to be on the safe side. Once these women are taken they are already lost to us. If they eat, drink, then it's too late. We have to stop them going with him. We need to hammer it home harder, make them scared to be honest."

Bob Scunthorpe sniffed, he nodded. "Are you thinking television?"

"Yes, sir. Television, as a matter of urgency, the news bulletins as soon as possible, the websites, Facebook pages, Twitter. But..." She took in a breath. He waited. "The biggest problem as I see it is that we need help from the public. We still need to be able to approach people in the services, give them the opportunity to come to us, talk to us. We need to warn them, and we need to use them, make them think. We really need to make everyone take this more seriously."

He nodded, steepled his hands on the desk in front of him. She was going to have to spell it out.

"Thing is, sir, we need to warn young women not to talk to male police officers. Not to go off with people who tell them that they are with the force. As well as that, we have to face the fact that it could be..." She paused. "We have tried not to acknowledge it, but it could be that he is one of us. With all the television, films, and books about these days, I think the public know as much about policing as we do ourselves, or at least they think they do, so it's still highly likely that this is someone passing himself off as some kind of official. But I do think that we have to consider the unpalatable possibility that it might be a serving officer."

He was already shaking his head, "If the press got hold of that they'd crucify us. We need to think very carefully before saying anything. It would cause considerable ill feeling among our fellow officers for a start and, though we want the public aware, we don't want them overly suspicious. We have enough problems with distrust at the best of times, and this is certainly not the best of times." He looked saddened, a little shocked. He pushed it aside. "For the moment we'll get on with the rest of it, the television appeal. If that helps, and if it does turn out to be someone in the force we'll deal with that robustly, but let's not look for trouble. However, all that said, there is another matter." He coughed, looked down at his desk. Tanya knew what was coming, her stomach clenched.

"We have decided that we need to move this up a notch." He glanced at her, "I'm sure you've realised that this has now become a major crime."

"Yes sir."

"For the moment, obviously we have to carry on, we have to keep looking for this poor girl. But, I would ask that you make everything ready to hand this over. I'm sorry Tanya, but they are preparing a team from the Major Crime Unit to come in after the weekend."

"Yes, sir." There was nothing more that she could say, her throat had closed over with disappointment. He carried on, telling her that it was no reflection on what she had done, that it was policy, but his words were white noise. She had failed.

She couldn't argue with him. She shook herself mentally. Jane was missing, she had to save her, he had said they must carry on. She took a breath, got a grip. "In the meantime, sir, I would like officers at the services, all of them if we can manage it, but at least the two where we've had disappearances and the other one going south. I would like them all to be women. We need to catch people who use the cafés, the shops, even the parking, we need to find out if anyone else has been approached, but we can't do it with men. We can't send out such a conflicting message."

"Have you any idea what a can of worms that would be, Tanya? In this day and age, can you imagine the backlash? Apart from anything else I don't even know if we can spare that number of female officers, the logistics alone would be a nightmare. We have spent years integrating, years, and now you are asking me to allocate duties using gender as a criterion? The press would have a field day."

"Yes, sir." There was nothing else she could say. She gulped and folded her hands in her lap, waiting for him to tell her that she was mad, that they would wait to make those decisions until other people had taken over, someone with more of an idea.

He didn't do that. "Leave this with me. I have noted everything you've said. I need to speak to the Assistant Chief Constable."

Chapter 29

She walked down the corridor struggling with clashing thoughts. Had she screwed this up so badly that her career would be over just as it was taking off? She remembered the conversation with Kate, that woman had accepted that there were to be no more promotions, but didn't mind, she had everything else: husband, kids, the sport. If Tanya didn't have this, what was left?

She turned into the incident room, Paul glanced up, shook his head. "I'm trying, boss, but the badge is unclear, and there are a lot that are similar. I need to find that first. I'll do it." She nodded at him, gave him a smile.

"Right, the rest of you, anything?" For now, she wouldn't share the news. She didn't want them to lose the impetus. There was still time, and anyway, when she did have to hand it over, it had to be clear that she had done everything she could, that there was no room for criticism of any of them. She glanced at Sue and wondered if she would gloat. That smarted as much as the rest of it.

A charity shop manager thought he might recognise the dress, but it had been months ago, the guy had paid in cash and when they sent the image to see if he could identify the customer, he wouldn't commit himself.

According to what he was told at the time, the dress had been bought for the man's daughter. He remembered, because he had congratulated him on the upcoming wedding, but it turned out the girl was involved in re-enactment. The dress fitted the look she wanted, a medieval princess. The manager had been intrigued and looked it up on line. It was ridiculous in his opinion, grown men fighting with swords, and not real swords at that.

"He didn't say that, did he?" Charlie looked horrified.

"Yeah, he did. I think he must be a Game of Thrones fan. If it's not some sort of exotic steel with a razor-sharp edge, it's not worth bothering with." Dan grinned, "Apparently, he had a laugh about it, but then they realised that it would be a good marketing angle, so they printed out some of the pictures and stuck them up around the shop.

"Have you got his home address?"

Dan nodded. "Get down there, will you Dan? Take Sue with you. Have a look at the images anyway, but more important, see if you can't pin him down a bit; if we can get an idea of when, we can see what re-enactment events there were in the area. We might spot the dress. I mean surely if he had a trawl around the internet, the record will be on his machine. If he doesn't play ball, confiscate the thing and bring it back here for the IT department. Try to pin him down to some sort of description if you can, anything could be a help. Great work, Dan." She thought he would burst into flames, he went so red.

"Charlie."

He nodded and headed to their office. She looked at the clock. It was already past eight, how long could she expect them to work? This was another lead, she was fired up, she glanced through the window into the room. Dan and Sue were already on the way, Paul had his head down, scrolling images on his screen, Kate was on the phone.

Yes, they would stay. It had been the right decision not to tell them yet.

Charlie spent the next half an hour in silence, there was just the click of his mouse, the rattle of the scroll wheel. Tanya read through her notes, walked into the incident room, and updated the boards. She dragged out a new one and pinned Jane Mackie's picture to the top.

Charlie looked up as she went back into the office, he pushed his chair away from the desk, stretched his arms above his head, and groaned. "Well I have to say they are a strange bunch these 're-enactors' but I think some of them are probably really knowledgeable about history. It looks as though it's quite fun in a way. Camping, dressing up, it's family stuff you know?"

"I don't know if I see this bloke as a family man though, Charlie. Where is he keeping the women? Not in a semi in Oxford I shouldn't think. Wouldn't your wife think it was odd if you were in late, out early?"

He tipped his head to one side, glanced at his watch and grinned. She threw her pen at him.

It missed.

Chapter 30

Dan and Sue came back at just after ten. The shop manager's computer had given them a sales date in the previous June. He couldn't be specific but had looked at the sites in the days immediately after the dress had been sold. They had printed out some of the images to give the team an idea of what they were looking at, but there were none like that of the silver, sequinned dress pinned to the board. There were many of women, long skirts trailing in the mud, cooking over open fires, standing on the sidelines cheering on their knights. The more they looked at it the less appealing it seemed to Tanya, mud and discomfort held no allure, but then there was no accounting for people's tastes and it was innocent enough.

Everyone was exhausted, it was time to call it a night. It made more sense to have an early start. As they left the quiet building, Tanya took a last look at the new photograph, the face of Jane Mackie. She turned away and switched out the light. She had no idea what the girl might be going through, but each passing hour took her further and further from salvation and it was very probably too late already. She was swept by a feeling of impotence and hopelessness.

Paul was already in the office before seven, he was on the phone when Tanya arrived. She'd brought breakfast from the café down the road – pastries and coffee. He covered the mouthpiece with his hand as she dropped the bags on the table in the corner. "I've got the regiment, I'm on to them now. I want to send a picture of that soldier over as soon as I find where best to send it."

"Brilliant. Well done, Paul." She grinned at him, carried over the extra-large latte and placed it on his desk. She could have kissed him but had to make do with a warm croissant, a thumbs up and a beaming smile.

Dan was red eyed and tired, he had spent hours into the early morning peering at even more images of re-enactors. There had been a few gatherings since the dress had been sold, thousands of pictures and videos, but there had been no sign of it. "The thing is," he told them, "so many of the women wear cloaks and shawls and what have you, it might be hard to spot it even if it is there. Anyway, I've got a mate in the computer section and he has some software that might help. I'm seeing him later, he can take the image and then search for it all over the internet. He's coming in early to set it going."

They were pulling out all the stops. "Brilliant, thanks guys. We've got to have some luck soon, I just hope it's soon enough for Jane." Inadvertently, carelessly, she'd lowered the mood, she could have bitten off her tongue.

"Well, I wish I had some better news," Kate shook her head as she spoke, "I've had no luck at all with the motorway cameras. I think you were right, he's thrown Millie's phone out when he's been in the middle of traffic."

Tanya nodded, "If you decided to go off with someone, someone who had convinced you that they were in the police, what sort of vehicle would you expect them to have?"

Kate responded, "Well a patrol car obviously, but we already know which ones were in the area, we've done that check haven't we? Could be an unmarked car, could be a personnel carrier. A four-wheel drive, one of those bloody big black things." As she spoke Tanya remembered the traffic officer, she must check with Charlie about that, but he'd put nothing on the board.

"Can you have another look at the recordings, make a note of anything that looks even vaguely like a police vehicle. It's a long shot I know but... well, something might stand out. Let's get on with it. Oh, and keep up with monitoring those tweets and Facebook posts if you can, contact us straight away if there are more angel references, I'm sure there's something important there. If it all gets too much let me know and I'll try and get you some help."

Kate nodded and turned back to her computer, Tanya could tell by the set of her shoulders there would be no request for help.

* * *

Jane cowered in the corner, the rattle of the ladder and the clump of his feet on the rungs had sent her scurrying across the rough boards. She closed her eyes.

When they had pulled into the messy yard she had tried to drag the sliding door open, but the child lock was on. He'd left her there, screaming in the back of the van, hammering on the windows. She'd climbed into the front but, of course, he'd taken the key with him.

When he came back he brought a length of rope. She thought he might strangle her, had screamed and cried, clambered back over the seats to hide in the narrow space. He slid open the door, grabbed her leg and twisted until she had no choice but to turn onto her belly. She kicked out, felt her foot connect with the flab of his stomach, heard him grunt, but he ignored her feeble struggles. He wrapped the rope round and round her arms, pinning them to her chest, down and down, holding her legs with his knees, down and down, until she was a cocoon, writhing and twisting in the gap between the rear seat and the back of the cab. He pulled her forward and hoisted her to his shoulders. She screamed and wriggled but it did no good. He was stronger than she was, much stronger.

He carted her up the short ladder and clambered into the loft space dropping her on the floor. He'd untied her then and reached out to smooth down her hair. She'd flinched away from his touch, crabbed back into the corner, buried her head between her bent knees, sobbing.

After a few minutes standing over her he went back, disappeared through the hatchway, pulling it down behind him.

All the time, through the whole episode he had cried, he had apologised to her over and over and over; he was sorry for scaring her, sorry for hurting her.

* * *

"I've brought you something to eat. You need to eat this." He pushed a tray across the floor, it was covered with a cloth, she could smell the food. Her mouth watered in spite of herself, her stomach rumbled.

He didn't stay, but when he went he left the light on, a single bulb fastened into a socket, high up in the eaves. She crawled across and pulled the cloth away. There were two bottles of water, she snatched one of them up, peeled the plastic from around the top, and gulped it down greedily. There was a plate holding a bread roll and a bowl with some thin soup in it. Vegetable pieces floated in the liquid.

Chapter 31

"I've found him." Paul hadn't bothered to knock, he waved the picture of the soldier in the air. "I sent over the CCTV image, it wasn't that clear, but they went through their records, found out who was on leave this last Friday, or travelling to new postings et cetera, and then went through any likely candidates. They weren't keen to give out information at first, but I told them the situation, I didn't have a choice. Anyway, they've spoken to his mate, apparently there were a few of them in the service area that day, but this one was in the café and remembers the girl."

Tanya leapt from her chair, "So, what's the deal? Who is he, where is he and how soon can we speak to him? We'll need a police artist. Charlie can you get on to that? Paul, you and me will go and take him with us."

"His name is Connolly, he's a sergeant, but it's not that simple."

"Why? What's not simple?"

"They were heading for Hereford."

"And."

"Hereford."

"Yeah, you said – Hereford, and?"

Paul glanced at Charlie, who nodded at him. "Hereford, Tanya. The Regiment."

"Oh, right. SAS. But, I don't see why that's a problem."

Paul stepped further into the office, "It's not really. It's just that he'll have to come here when they find him. They don't want us going there."

"Find him? And anyway, what do you mean they don't want us there? We're the bloody police."

He shrugged his shoulders. "They're on it. They know it's urgent. They said a few hours at most and they'll bring him here. He's somewhere out training, or god knows what, and they aren't going to say."

There was nothing more she could do to make it happen faster. She rang the Chief Inspector's office and asked to see him.

He was in a meeting. She slammed the phone down, just a bit too hard. Charlie frowned at her. They had started so well, she had felt the hope rise and now every turn seemed to be barred. She took a couple of deep breaths. This wasn't professional, it was wrong. She nodded to Charlie watching from his side of the room. Managed a grin. "Sorry." He shook his head, smiled back at her, and went to turn on the kettle.

The army were as good as their word and by twelve o'clock the soldier was being shown to an interview suite. He was in civvies, fit and young, with a shaved head. He had obviously been briefed about why he had been brought there and had come ready to take care of business. He had already jotted down what he could remember. In his hand was a notebook with the times, the exact location, even what the girl had on the plate in front of her.

"She looked pretty brassed off." He laughed. "Reminded me of my kid sister. I gave her a wink, but you know, had to just be a bit careful. Didn't want to give her the wrong idea. Then the bloke turned up. Well, at first I thought it was her dad, obviously, but then it looked as though they were arguing. I went over. It was a copper, he showed me his warrant card, and I left them to it. I reckoned she was probably a runaway." He stopped, rubbed his hands over his face. "I am so sorry. I honestly didn't realise. She was just a kid, you know a teenager – glowering and being antsy."

"It's okay, it's okay, Sergeant Connolly. It's not your fault. But you can help us now and we need to move pretty fast. Do you think you could work with the police artist? Give us a good idea of what he looks like. We have CCTV footage but none of it is clear, he's clever at hiding his face."

"Please call me Trevor. Absolutely, anything I can do. I didn't get a long look at him, but I'll do my best. I feel so bloody pissed about this. That poor kid. I can't believe I let this happen."

"You didn't, you didn't let it happen. Don't beat yourself up about it. Just get to work and get me a likeness I can use. You're our best hope up to now, we need your help to find him and to get the word out, to make sure he can't do this to anyone else."

Tanya nodded at Charlie, he was already opening the interview suite door. "This way, Trevor, I'll take you down to see the police artist."

She listened as they strode away down the corridor, the young soldier still apologising. If they were too late, which surely they were going to be, he would have to live with this for the rest of his life. She knew he was tough, he must be to follow that profession, but she had seen the pain in his eyes and knew that he would carry the guilt for a long time.

She picked up the phone, rang through to Bob's secretary. "I need to have a word, quickly if I can. Is he out of his meeting?"

"On his way back right now. If you come along, you can wait for him."

She felt the change, the tension eased, the way seemed a tiny bit easier.

Chapter 32

Tanya followed Bob Scunthorpe into his office. She didn't sit, she wanted to cut this as short as possible, needing to get back to the team.

He slid in behind his desk, opened the file and then looked at her. "I've just been with the Assistant Chief Constable." He grinned. "He's at home today, as you'd expect. Anyway, what we are going to do is assign mixed teams." He held up a hand as she moved forward on her chair, prepared to argue. "It's not politically sound to segregate male and female officers. It sends out all sorts of messages, the media would have a field day. 'Can't we trust our own men to work alone' and so on. Now we both know that it's rubbish. We both know the reasoning. But it's sticky and difficult. So, we are going to assign mixed teams to stick together, joined at the hip." He gave a wry smile. "It's going to play havoc with my overtime budget, but it can't be helped. We are going live on television in…" he glanced at his watch, "about an hour, and we are putting it out there that members of the public must avoid speaking to officers alone. We are not going to specify male. However, we need an image to go along with this. I believe you have some CCTV that is unclear but does definitely show it's a man we are dealing with."

"We have a witness, sir."

He looked up at her now, his face alive with interest.

"He's with the police artist right now, we should have a good likeness quite soon. I like this witness, he's switched on and clever, and he is tormented because he didn't do more to help Jane."

"Wonderful. Well done, Tanya. Well done."

"It was DS Harris who found him, sir." He nodded, approved of her honesty. "I think he worked most of last night. The team are working their butts off." She blushed as she realised what she had said. Bob just grinned and moved on.

"I know they are, and I'm sorry about what's happened with this but at least when you hand it over, you'll have nothing to reproach yourself with. Right, so, you haven't done a live press conference before, I don't think."

She shook her head.

"I'd like you on this with me. I'll do most of the talking. It can be a bit daunting, they have the manners of farmyard animals. We won't take questions, but you put together a list of the things you want to get across, we'll get our heads down with the chap from the Press Office, knock it into shape and so on. I'll meet you downstairs at half past one. Well done."

She strode back down the corridor, ran down the stairs, her mind whirling, she mustn't miss anything, she had to get this right. She had to protect all those other women. It was the weekend, the motorways were busy. They hadn't found Jane yet, but he had taken Millie while he still held Sarah. She had to get this right.

She stopped by the locker room and grabbed her blue blazer. It was smarter than the puffa jacket she had worn to work. She picked up the new boots. Would Bob notice if she changed her shoes, would he think her vain, shallow?

She stroked the fine, soft leather, sighed, and pushed them back into the metal cabinet. She went next door, into the ladies, ran a comb through her hair and pulled it back, away from her face. She gathered it into a pony tail and then wound it round a couple of times until it was a neat bun. She pulled a few strands loose, curling around her face. She slapped on a tiny bit of lipstick, not enough to notice if you were a man, but enough to brighten her face for the cameras. She smoothed down her skirt and had a quick turn back and forth in front of the long mirror. She would do.

She dragged out her mobile, phoned Charlie, and brought him up to date. She would have to tell him soon about the Major Crime Team; she should have done it already, but it was too embarrassing.

He promised to move the artist along but warned her that he didn't think there was enough time to have anything ready before the broadcast. "You'll have to use the stills from the CCTV for now and tell them there'll be a better image soon. We can email it to the media offices and print hard copies for anyone who can wait." He told her that the soldier was proving pretty sure of himself and they already had a decent start. "Later we need to have a word about George Simpson. He hasn't come back from his days off, and he hasn't been in touch with anyone. Trouble is this picture isn't looking anything like him."

She made a note. Could there be more than one man involved with this?

* * *

The whirr and flash of cameras wasn't completely new, she had seen it before, had waited on the sidelines while her last boss had done just what she was doing now. The Chief Inspector had been right in his assessment of the press pack; they yelled, waved their arms about, jostled and pushed against each other. They needed them though, to make this work. Bob Scunthorpe had his say. He outlined the disappearances, the discoveries of both bodies, the concern about Jane Mackie. He deliberately kept some things back, he didn't mention the tinsel, it was unlikely that the poor old man who had discovered Millie would have noticed it, and it had fallen to the floor in the graveyard where they had found Sarah. They did have images of the dresses, it was possible someone would recognise their wedding dress, after all. It might give them a narrower area of search.

He turned to Tanya, and nodded.

She held up the image from the closed-circuit cameras and apologised for the quality. She stressed they were preparing an image that would be much more reliable and to make sure that the press office had the email addresses for it to be sent on. "There will be hard copies available as well. All I can do is ask that you be patient. We need it to be as recognisable as it can be, but we will have it ready within the next hour." She crossed her fingers mentally as she put a time constraint on the work that the artist was doing.

When they released that, surely something would break. They were prepared for the fact that a lot of people would call about innocent men, either because they had a grudge, or were simply mistaken. They had to weed them out, they had to pick out the weirdos and the attention seekers, the ones who didn't understand that tying up the civilian call takers, jamming the phone lines, could have terrible consequences; that someone with genuine information may give up if they couldn't get through.

First though, they had to get the image finished and she was itching to get back to the office, to call and chivvy them along. She paused a moment, waited to gain their full attention, then repeated what Bob had said about police officers only working in pairs. "This man is very dangerous. We believe that he has been responsible for the deaths of two women and the abduction of a third. I want to stress to the public, especially women alone using the motorway services, that you will not be approached by a

142

lone police officer." She had been told to avoid using gender references wherever possible. "If anyone has been approached by an individual who made them uneasy, or saw anything at all that seemed suspicious – in the toilets, the shops, cafés or parking areas – please contact us. A young girl's life may well depend on information that you have. Please come forward if you have anything that you think may be of help. But it is just as important that you stay safe. Police officers will not ask you to go with them and they absolutely will not ask you to go with them alone. Please take care."

* * *

Bob Scunthorpe held out a hand. She knew that in past times he would probably have given her a quick hug, patted her shoulder, but physical contact was a minefield. He did beam at her though, and told her that she had done a sterling job. He was proud of her.

"Thank you, sir. Let's hope it gets a result."

She couldn't wipe the grin from her face as she ran back up the stairs.

She went immediately into the incident room. "Well done everybody. I know how hard you're working but it's paying off. Thank you." She went back to her office, called Pizza Hut and ordered up lunch for everyone. It was the least she could do, it was team building.

Her team.

She phoned Charlie, "How's it coming?"

"Nearly there I think. We're printing out a copy now."

"What has he said, the soldier?"

"Well you know how it is, he didn't see him for long, and he dismissed him when he thought he was official. I reckon he's done his best. We can never really know, not until we catch someone, but I should think that if you knew the guy, and this is close to right, you'd recognise him."

Chapter 33

Jane knew she could go two days without eating. It was easy, she'd done it before, many times. If she had water she could do more, she did three once, nearly four. Three full days and then her mum had insisted they go out to eat. She threw up afterwards but it had broken the run.

She knew she would be dizzy, that she would feel weak, but that didn't matter. Water filled her belly and eased the feelings of hunger. She didn't even want anything yet.

She'd used the bucket in the corner, she knew that was what it was for because there was a roll of toilet paper on the floor beside it. That was another advantage of not eating. The bucket smelled faintly of bleach but that was okay because it was a clean smell. The bucket had been blue but now there were pale streaks on it. She'd felt a chill ripple down her spine. Had there been someone else, some other woman using this, sitting here where she was? Had he kept them until the bucket overflowed?

She had crawled around the loft, pulled and poked at anything that looked as though it might be loose, might give her access to the outside. She had shouted. Before she had peed in the bucket she had used it to rattle on the boards in the roof. It was plastic and cheap, it made a noise but wasn't tough enough to batter a hole through, nothing like that. She heard the birds cooing. Pigeons, she thought, and when she shouted she heard them fly away and then, when they felt brave enough, they came back again. She kept doing it, scaring them away. Maybe someone would notice and wonder what they were afraid of. There was nothing here but the papier-mâché tray, the flimsy bowl. The plastic spoon had broken as soon as she had tried to dig around the edge of the trap door. She still had one bottle of water, she needed to save that until the hunger began. She had no idea how to do anything to save herself. She was so bloody stupid. Stupid and useless.

She heard the ladder and backed herself into the corner. She clenched her fists and straightened her shoulders. She was in no doubt that this asshole could overpower her easily, but she would go down fighting. She would never be able to live with herself if she didn't fight; if he raped her, she would at least have done her best and that had to be good. They had a woman visit school one time. She had been raped and she said that the thing that ate at her — that was what she had said '*ate at her*' — was that she thought she should have fought more. '*Give it everything*,' she had said, '*you have everything to lose*'.

His head poked above the hole in the floor. She should have gone over there, she could have stamped on him. Next time, if there was a next time, that's what she would do; she'd stamp on his head, jump on him, force him off the ladder. She'd kick him and stamp on his face and then she would run. But this time it was too late. She was in the corner and he was there, coming up through the hole.

He stopped with his head and shoulders poking up like a whack-a-mole, looked at the tray, and sighed. "You didn't eat the soup."

"I'm not eating your stinking soup, asshole. You can take the soup and stick it up your arse."

145

He shook his head. "You need to eat something. It will help. We won't move on until you eat something. You can't go home until then. I'll make you something else. I'll make you an omelette. You'd probably like that better."

"Piss off with your omelette, you pig, I'm not eating anything. They'll be looking for me now. My dad will be looking for me and when he gets his hands on you, he'll turn you into a friggin' omelette." She felt the rage building, like nothing she had experienced before, fizzing in her nerve endings, clutching at her gut. She pushed away from the wall and ran across the boards. She kicked out, as hard as she could, aiming for his ugly, stupid head.

He'd taken her shoes. As he ducked away below the level of the trap door, her bare toes collided with the edge of the hole. She felt the bones in her foot snap, heard the crack somewhere inside herself. She screeched, as her stomach roiled and tears filled her eyes. She fell to the floor rolling and groaning. The world was a blur of agony. The edges of her vision darkened, the room, the horror, the man, receded, and she fell into the blackness.

When she awoke it was dark, it was the pain that made her aware. He'd turned the light out and all there was to illuminate the space was leaking in through the edges of the roof where the tiles had moved. Her foot was swollen to twice its normal size, it throbbed and ached and when she tried to move, pain shot right through her body and nausea and faintness threatened again. She lay where she was on the dirty, dusty boards and let the tears roll across her face and drip onto the floor.

She managed to turn onto her back but that was the extent of it. She couldn't move her leg without shards of agony. She was lost. Now, she wouldn't jump on him, she wouldn't kick him down the stairs, she wouldn't run from this place. She hadn't even had the satisfaction of hurting him and she knew that now she would never be able to get away. She screamed, an animal cry of terror and desperation, and she heard the birds leave the roof with a clatter of wings. She lay back and wanted to die.

Chapter 34

Tanya heard Charlie in the incident room. She looked through her office window to watch as he pinned the picture onto the board they had set up for Jane Mackie. The team clustered around.

Back in the office he slumped in his chair. "We're sending off the digital copies. As soon as we've printed them we've got patrol cars taking them to the services, we're going to do the town centre as well. It's a good picture. I think that definitely if you know this guy you would recognise him. 'Course we are relying on Sergeant Connolly's memory being good. Fingers crossed."

"Have you got one?" Tanya held out her hand.

"Sorry, I just pinned one up, I left some on the table out there." He turned to the door, but she stopped him.

"I'll go and look out there, it's okay," Tanya said.

The team were still examining the board, Paul turned when Tanya walked up behind him, "You know he looks like a sergeant I worked with a couple of years ago. Transferred to Yorkshire."

"Really, can you remember his name?"

There was silence, the tension in the room was building as they acknowledged the idea that this could turn out to be a colleague after all.

"Keiran, yes that was it. Keiran Laing. Older than me, similar build to him in the CCTV and he had those eyes; a bit slitty, aren't they?"

"Are you sure enough for me to take this to Bob Scunthorpe, Paul? It's quite an accusation."

"I'm pretty sure." He seemed to be wavering and they all felt for him. If what he was saying was true, the repercussions would be awful; if he was making a mistake it would be even worse.

"Tell you what, I've got a mate up there. Why don't I send him the picture through and just ask him if he thinks it looks like anyone? Not lead him on, you know. Let him decide."

"Do we want to involve other officers? How well did you know him?"

"Pretty well, it does look like him. You know if someone had asked 'Who's this?' that's who I would have said."

Tanya spoke again, "Are you sure enough for me to take this to the Chief Inspector?"

Paul looked tormented, "I suppose, but..." He paused and looked around the group. "Okay. Let me put it this way, if he wasn't on the job, I'd be pretty sure."

She went back into the office and put in a call.

As she waited for Glenys to ring her back she stood gazing at the image, Charlie stood behind her. "It's good isn't it?" he said. "So much better these days with the computer imaging. They look like real people."

Tanya didn't answer, but took a step nearer, peering up at the print out. She reached for it and pulled out the push pins.

"Trouble is that they are a bit everyman aren't they, unless there's something outstanding, a mole or a scar. See, in spite of what Paul's just said, I have the feeling that I've seen him, Charlie." As she spoke she looked up at him, her forehead creased, she was chewing the side of her lip. "I've seen him somewhere, or someone who looks awfully like him anyway."

"Someone you've worked with?" Charlie dreaded the answer.

She shook her head vigorously, "No, not that. Recently. Somewhere, hell, I should be able to remember." She scratched at her hair, closed her eyes. "Damn it won't come. I wonder if it was one of the charity shops, it was something like that."

"Best thing is let it stew a bit, think about something else, that's what I find and then it'll come to you."

She nodded at him, picked up one of the extra pictures, took it back into her office and propped it against her monitor. By now the email had come from the sketch artist and she enlarged it until it filled her screen.

Charlie made them coffee. "Right, so, the service area manager. He should have been back in work yesterday afternoon, after his day off. He didn't show, and they haven't been able to contact him."

Tanya turned away from her study of the computer, "What do we know about him? Apart from him being a greasy, icky little man with obvious male chauvinist leanings."

Charlie handed her a printed record of George Simpson's brief brush with the authorities in the north east, near Newcastle. There had been nothing since then.

"It's not much is it, and there was doubt about it all. Maybe he was genuinely caught short, perhaps his car did break down." She shrugged, and then her eyes widened, "That's it – bloody hell that's who it was."

"Nah, as I said it doesn't look like him. Not really. Same sort of age I guess, as far as we can tell, but the hair's wrong and…"

He was interrupted by the phone ringing and Tanya's conversation with Bob Scunthorpe. It was difficult, and she blew out a breath as she put down the handset. "He's going to contact Yorkshire, find out where this Keiran is at the moment. Christ, I hope we're wrong, but I've put my head on the block a bit now."

She pointed at the screen, "I don't mean Simpson. The bloke that came to his office, shit what was his name? It was after you went out. Someone pushed his way in and the assistant manager sent him away. He was a friend of Simpson or something, somebody who did casual work for him." She thumped the desk, the noise turning the heads of the rest of the team in the other office. "Peter. That's what it was. Peter. No surname I don't think. We need to find him. What else do we know about Simpson? Apart from the fact that he might be a flasher and use prossies?"

"Well, I guess we should give him the benefit of the doubt especially with the rest of it."

"What's the rest of it then?"

"He lives in Wheatley, on his own as far as I could find out. Doesn't socialise at work much. But here's the oddity. He's a lay minister."

Tanya shook her head, puzzled. "Which means, what?"

"Well he's not like a priest or a vicar exactly, but he goes and preaches. Like a volunteer I think. Methodist."

"Methodist?"

Charlie nodded.

"I don't know much about all that stuff. We never had much religion."

Charlie grinned at her. "My granny made sure we had our share. I still go sometimes, to church you know. I like the singing, the getting together."

"So, Methodists. They have angels, right?"

He nodded, scrolled through some sites that he'd been researching. He turned his screen so that she could read the article he had been looking at. "Yeah, they're pretty big on angels."

She nodded at him. "Have we got his address? This ties in with what I was told: charity work. The assistant manager at the services said this Peter helped with charity work. We need to find him, and the quickest way is going to be interfering with Simpson's little holiday. Come on."

They collected their coats, called into the incident room to let the team know where they were going and set off to have a word with the missing minister.

Tanya's phone was on hands-free so they both heard the relief in Bob Scunthorpe's voice when he told them that they could discount Officer Laing. He was invalided out with multiple sclerosis and used a wheelchair. They called the office to let a very relieved Paul know.

Chapter 35

George lived on the top floor of a three-story block. It was part of a short terrace built to give the appearance of tall houses, but they were obviously flats. Brick-built with chipped and peeling wood under the windows, it was drab and dull. It had probably originally been council property but 'for sale' signs indicated private ownership of at least some of them. The frontage had been concreted at some stage to provide parking, but it was crumbling at the joints and edges, weeds poking through. Green wheelie bins lined the space under the ground floor windows and recycling boxes were tucked into alcoves holding electric meters. Tanya peered up at the curtains drawn across the windows of what would be his flat and rang the bell. They couldn't hear the chime but the small light behind the plastic cover flickered.

While they waited she turned, jigged from foot to foot, and stepped back to peer at the upper floor. Opposite, across the narrow road, was a row of flat-roofed, lock up garages. A couple of them had cars parked on the slab in front. It was Saturday afternoon, there were kids playing outside in the street, cars driving back and forth, teens on bikes. It was all very ordinary. It occurred to Tanya that probably none of these people were giving any thought to two dead women and a missing girl and yet it was such a short distance away. They must have all used the motorway, most of them stopping at the services. Small happenings, everyday things, but when they went wrong the repercussions were terrible.

She rang the bell again. Charlie had walked to the end of the terrace. He disappeared down the side. She heard his voice, another male answering. With a final quick glance upwards, she joined him around the corner.

The man Charlie was talking to was middle-aged, wearing jeans and an old, comfortable-looking sweatshirt. He had a baseball cap on with some sort of logo on the front. He'd been decorating, or cleaning windows and, as they chatted, he fiddled with a wet rag clutched in his hands, twisting it repeatedly. Charlie still had his warrant card in his hand, so he had obviously taken the conversation to an official level. Tanya stood quietly, it was enough to listen, she didn't need to join in.

The man shook his head. "No, I don't think he's away, as such. There was music; hymns. He's some sort of a vicar or something in his spare time. We don't have a lot to do with each other, but he's no bother."

"When did you hear the music? Was that today?"

Another shake of the head, a downturn of the thin, dry lips. "Nah, not today. Haven't heard or seen him today, nor yesterday now you mention it. So, I suppose it was Thursday. Yeah. Thursday night. Quite late."

"Thanks for that." Charlie held out his hand, but the other man grinned and wagged the dripping cloth at him.

"No problem, mate. Oh, that's his car there, the blue one, in front of his garage. I reckon he must be in then. He doesn't walk anywhere as far as I can see. Not in trouble, is he?"

"No, we just needed a word that's all."

"Right." He turned back to his cleaning.

With Tanya in the lead they went back to the front of the building, rang the bell again. There was still no response. They crossed the road and peered into the car, it was very ordinary. There was a sticker of a fish on the rear wing but that was the only overt indication of his religious affiliation. They rattled at the metal door of the garage. Charlie twisted the handle, but it was pointless because, as well as the lock integral to the handle, there was a padlock threaded through an extra hasp and staple screwed to the frame. It seemed that security might be a priority for George.

None of the others had extra locks and a couple of the doors were slightly open. It was the weekend, people were likely working with their tools, out on bikes. But not George.

It was one of the middle garages, there was no window. Charlie strode along the front, stepping aside to avoid a pool of oil, a couple of fast food cartons, and something else that looked like the results of overindulgence by someone the night before. The pavement down the narrow side passage was cracked and uneven, he had to steady himself with a hand against the wall as he made his way to the back. There were small square windows in the back of the block, one for each unit. A couple of them were broken and he had forgotten to count which one had been pointed out as George Simpson's.

He was tired, he was becoming less efficient. He sighed. It couldn't be helped: a sleepless baby, worry about his wife and the pressure of this case, what did he expect?

Angry with himself he stomped back to the front, counted down the doors. Tanya was trying the boot of the blue car, but of course, that too was locked.

Eventually he was able to peer into the rear window of George Simpson's garage with his hands either side of his head cutting out the light. The ill-fitting front door let in a sliver of daylight, but it was grey and dim inside. He squinted through the grubby glass expecting general junk, same as his own place and all those of his mates.

It was too dark to see clearly, but the place was tidy. There was a bench, or a table, with a chair in front of it. There was equipment of some sort, looked like a computer. Around the wall were shelves with boxes piled on top of each other. More boxes were on the floor. It was neat.

Tanya joined him, he stood aside to let her have a look. She pulled a torch from her shoulder bag and tried to shine it through the window but all that happened was that the light reflected on the grimy glass making it even more difficult to see anything. She turned to him, frowning. "What do you reckon?"

"Well, no answer from his flat, his car out front, the fact that nobody has seen him, though all indications are that he's there – it's odd. It's unsettling. I can't make out what's going on here." He indicated the grubby rear of the lock up.

Tanya nodded, turned, and went back to the front of the flats. "Try his phone again. Have you got his landline number?"

Charlie nodded, and dialled. They heard the phone ring out, the sound faint through the closed windows. "Try his mobile, though to be honest unless it's on the window ledge I don't reckon we'd hear it." They didn't.

"I could call and arrange for a warrant to search." Tanya had taken out her mobile.

"It's the weekend."

"Are you worried about Mr Simpson, Charlie?"

He knew what he was supposed to say. They wanted to go inside but to do that they had to be able to say that they believed he was in danger. "Hang on." He held up a hand and went back around the corner.

The man with the bucket and rags had moved to the rear of the terrace, there was a communal garden there, just a scraggy lawn, a couple of shrubs and a flower border with some petunias giving in to the end of the season.

"Hello mate. Sorry to bother you again."

The neighbour gave a start, dropped his bucket, splashing grey water on the flags. "Shit mate, you scared the living daylights out of me. I thought you'd gone."

"Sorry. It's just that we are a bit worried about Mr Simpson. You wouldn't know if anyone has a spare key for his flat, would you?" He'd taken out his warrant card again, held it by his side, a reminder that this was official business.

"Yeah, I should think Mrs Singh might well have one. She has one for me as well, most of us really. She's disabled, doesn't get out much so it's handy for tradesmen, stuff like that. Holidays, watering plants, well only on the ground floor obviously, but you know it's good isn't it, somebody having a spare?"

Charlie nodded.

"Gives her a chance to see someone, makes her feel useful." It was said in kindness, no sense of condescension. "She's two doors down from the entrance on the ground floor, she's got them grab handles beside her front door and a ramp for the chair."

"Brilliant. Thanks."

Mrs Singh was a plump Indian woman wearing a colourful sari. She had a bowl of keys on a shelf beside the front door. They showed her their identification and she rattled and riffled through them and then, with a huge grin, held out a key ring in the shape of a cross. Two keys jingled together as she leaned forward in her wheelchair to hand them over.

"Bloody hell, Tanya, there's so much wrong with that. She had keys for practically the whole block, she's vulnerable. That is such a bad idea."

"You could arrange for a crime prevention visit, but you know what, sometimes it's best to leave things alone.

She feels like she's helping, would you want to deprive her of that? It's obviously a decent little community."

Charlie sighed, "Yeah, I suppose you're right, in a way, but honestly it really worries me."

"I won't stand in your way if you want to do something about it, but let's just do this for now. I've got a bad feeling."

One key allowed them access through the front door. The narrow hallway was clean and there were a couple of prints on the walls in cheap frames. They climbed two flights of stairs.

At the top there was a tiny square landing and a wooden door with a small reinforced translucent window set in the upper panel. Tanya knocked hard three times, she called out, "Mr Simpson. Police. Could you open the door please?"

Charlie's phone rang. She turned to look at him, gave him a nod. He peered down, "Sorry." He swept his hand across the screen. "Granny. Can't talk right now. I'll call you back. Okay, okay yes, for sure."

Tanya smiled at him.

He looked sheepish, embarrassed. "I told her about the television thing. She wanted to know what you look like. I guess she wants to give me her opinion."

She raised her eyebrows at him, grinned and then turned back and knocked again on the door. "Mr Simpson, we have a key, we are coming in."

Chapter 36

The pain in Jane's foot was a dull ache; as long as she didn't try to move it she could cope without feeling sick. She had managed to slide across the rough floor so that she could lean her back against the wall. She didn't want to be right there, beside the trap door, if he came back. Didn't want to be within his reach. Maybe he wouldn't come back. Maybe she had made him so angry that he would just leave her there.

She wasn't that bothered any more. It was nearly dark, the pigeons had settled for the night, she had heard them scratching and cooing. She didn't frighten them away this time, they were a sort of company and anyway, it was mean, and she didn't want to be mean. If he didn't come back, and nobody found her, then she would die there. She would die of thirst when the water ran out. She looked at the bottle in her hand, tipped it to feel the liquid inside. There was probably just over a half left. What should she do? She could drink it all back now in a couple of big gulps. That was so tempting, she was very thirsty, but that would be it. Once it was gone she would start to die. She could make it last, take tiny little sips. She tipped the bottle again, she could probably make it last more than a day. She knew that she had plenty of self-control. But if she sipped it slowly would that be enough to keep her alive? Surely she had a set amount of water and whether she dripped it into her body slowly or took it all in one go, it would hardly make any difference. She pulled off the top, tipped the bottle and finished it.

She tossed the bottle aside. Carefully, favouring her injured foot, she slid to the floor, curled into a ball and closed her eyes.

She had no idea how long she slept, the light hadn't changed, so probably it wasn't very long. She was very uncomfortable, her hip and shoulder bones ached with the pressure of the hard wood and her neck was stiff. She didn't move, she listened. She heard him, he was moving about downstairs; if it was him. For a moment she wondered if it could be someone else, someone who was looking for her. Should she call out, hammer on the floor the way she had at first? She didn't have the energy and anyway, it was probably him. A couple of tears rolled across her cheek, she didn't bother about them.

She heard him on the ladder, lay still, what did any of it matter? She couldn't even be bothered to be afraid anymore.

He was hesitant, putting his head through the trap carefully, shining his torch around until he found her. She turned her face to look at him. He ran the cone of light across her body and then it came to rest on her injured foot. She was shocked at the sight of it. Her toes were swollen, and the bruising went as far as her ankle – black and dark bluey green, and angry red. She lifted her head to look at it. It didn't really look like her foot at all.

"Oh, look what you did." He sounded genuinely upset. She turned her head to look at his face but still made no effort to sit or move her body. "Why?" Surely, he didn't expect an answer. "You were perfect and now…" He shook his head. "I don't know what to do." Again, he looked at her, as if she could tell him.

"You could just let me go. Just let me go and I promise I won't tell anyone what you did. I can tell them I ran away." She didn't know where the idea came from, but as she said it she felt a stirring of hope. "You could help me down and then, well, either take me back to the café, or just leave me somewhere and I'll go home and say I ran away. They'll believe me. I've done it before."

He was shaking his head before she had finished speaking. "I don't think that's a good idea. I don't think you'd keep your promise. That's it you see. You don't keep your promises. You say you'll do something and then you don't. You say you'll stay and then you go away. Only angels keep their promises and angels are perfect. You're not perfect. You were, but…" He sighed again. "You can only be an angel if you're perfect." He lifted his hand and left two bottles on the floor beside the trap door "There's not much I can do for you now." He backed down the ladder closing the hatch and leaving her in the dark.

She slid on her behind to collect the bottles, tore off the plastic top and tipped the cool water into her mouth. She'd save the other one but this one was delicious. She felt drips on her chin, pulled the bottle away. The sides were wet, her hands were wet, how had she spilled it? She put it to her lips again, tipped it, more liquid dripped onto her chin. What was this? She held the bottle up, tilted it. Ran her fingers over the plastic. Just below the lid the outside of the bottle was moist, she held it over her hand, tilted it again. A small drop formed, dripped into her palm. There was a hole in the bottle, a tiny pin prick of a hole. She didn't know what it meant, but a chill ran through her. She had drunk more than half of the water. She thought for a moment, glanced around the dark space, sighed deeply, pulled the top off the bottle and poured the rest of it into her mouth. She leaned back against the wall. After a while, she felt no fear.

Chapter 37

Inside the front door of George Simpson's flat was a short, narrow hallway. They had pulled on blue gloves before they entered – routine nowadays.

There were a couple of photographs on the wall. One was an old studio portrait of a woman in dark clothes and a hat, stiff and self-conscious, the other was a young woman holding a baby. There was a row of hooks with two jackets and an umbrella hanging on them. The first door on the right led to a small square kitchen with fitted cupboards, a cooker, a fridge and a small table and chair under the window on the side of the building. It was clean; there was a mug beside the sink, but no other sign of occupation. They could see rows of houses and, in the distance, small hills, trees and fields. It was neither particularly pleasant nor unpleasant. It was bland.

The lounge was at the end of the hall, small and unremarkable. There was a religious painting on the wall. Tanya glanced at it. There was a three-piece suite in brown leather, a coffee table, and a desk in the corner with his computer and a bookshelf above it.

Charlie had gone the other way, into the room opposite the kitchen, and Tanya heard him stepping back along the fake wooden floor. She turned. He stood in the doorway, speechless for just a minute, he swallowed. "I wouldn't move anything. I've found him."

* * *

They went back outside, careful not to touch anything on the way, sat at the top of the stairs and made calls. It didn't take very long to set things in motion, there was no need for an ambulance or any sort of attempt at resuscitation. It was obvious that he was dead, no room for doubt. Tanya had gone back to stand at the bedroom door, to have a look around before the scene was handed over. There were empty pill packets on the bedside table; they didn't pick them up, it didn't matter to them what it was he had used, and for the moment things must be left as they were. He had vomited. It had spoiled the scene he had tried to create, wearing his suit with what she later discovered was called an alb, over the top. His religious garb. But he had not lain still and drifted peacefully away, his body had objected, his stomach revolted, and the result was sad and sordid. His eyes were wide and staring and devoid of light. He was gone.

While they waited for the medical examiner, the mortuary van, the SOCO team, there wasn't much they could say. Tanya's mind was whirling but none of it would settle. Uppermost was the idea that he could be their only link to the person who had killed twice, and abducted Jane. She went through what she could remember of their interviews with him, his difficult attitude. Had he been hiding a terrible crime, had he known what was happening? She hadn't thought so at the time, now she doubted her judgement. It would hardly show her in the best light if she'd been with him and had no inkling that he was any more than just a rather unpleasant character. She knew that often it was almost all instinct that pointed the way and if she didn't have that, she would never be among the best.

She went over the timeline in her head. She needed to get back and use the computer. He couldn't have been taking women from the services, he was well known to everyone who worked there – surely someone would have said something. Okay, the second woman had gone from a different one but Jane, she had been in the same place as Sarah. No, it wasn't possible. It was conceivable that he knew something about it all and it was possible that guilt had driven him to do what he had done. She couldn't have missed this.

"Did you see a note, Charlie?"

"Not from where I was. I didn't move anything to be honest. I could see there was nothing to be done and I didn't want to screw anything up. There was nothing on the dressing table, I know that for sure. There was a sort of wooden cross and that was it. The bedside table had a clock." He closed his eyes. "A book, I think it was a bible. I don't know if there was anything on the bed, I touched him briefly, and he was so cold, stiff, I knew he was dead, so I left him. We'll just have to wait."

"But he might have said something, in a note – something about Jane." She stood, sudden and urgent, stepped into the hallway and shouted to the technicians whom they could hear carefully and methodically cataloguing the contents and state of his room. Charlie had followed her in. "Don't close the bible. Hello, hey!"

A technician popped her head out of the bedroom. As she walked a little way down the hallway her bootees made soft noises on the fake wood, her trouser legs rubbed together rasping with every step. She didn't come out of the flat. "What?"

"There's a bible, on the bedside table. It's open."

"Oh yeah, I saw that."

"Don't close it, before you bag it up. I need to know what page it's open at." She turned to Charlie, "I need a suit."

Parked on the concrete apron was a van with a box of protective suits in the back, she grabbed one, stepped back into the hallway and pulled it on over her clothes.

The bible was as Charlie had seen it. She bent close to peer at the tiny writing. There was a piece of paper used as a book mark laid across the page. She had the technicians take pictures, they were defensive. "We would have done it as a matter of course. It's what we do." With a huff the woman turned away. She could tell that they thought she was overreacting to a suicide but wasn't going to spend time explaining herself. She reached out with a gloved hand and moved the bookmark. After unfolding it, she read out the short inscription. '*I'm sorry. I can't face the shame*'.

"'Exodus?' What's that Charlie? What's it about?"

"About the flight from Egypt."

"Okay. And does that say anything about committing suicide? I know for some religions it's a big no-no."

He leaned closer. "I can only remember bits, I just go to church for the singing you know, the social stuff. Granny would know probably but let's see. What chapter is it? Right. He tapped into his phone."

"We're ready to move the body now. Is there any reason why we can't?" a SOCO said.

Tanya held up a hand. "Just give me another minute. Anything Charlie?"

He showed her his phone, "The Ten Commandments."

"Right. Right, so that's about coveting goats and stuff, isn't it? What's the first one?"

"I am the Lord thy God and thou shalt have no other Gods before me." This came from a technician who was standing beside the door to the bathroom. "I studied them as part of my degree. It's difficult to see the relevance of a lot of it today, but basically it's just rules for decent behaviour I reckon."

Tanya screwed up her face, "Well that's not much help, I don't think. What else is there?"

He spoke again, happy to have a chance to show off a bit, "I think the one that most people think of as the most important is 'thou shalt not kill'. That's the one that gets quoted all the time."

She felt Charlie tense beside her.

"Look, I know it looks like a suicide, but it could be connected to something else. If you find any other notes let me know immediately, okay? And I need an address book. I need to find this man's friends pretty bloody quickly."

She saw the raised eyebrows, heard a huff of irritation – she'd annoyed them.

The woman SOCO spoke, "It could be there's something under the body, though I would be surprised. There's nothing in the bedroom, kitchen or living room that is obvious. It really does look as though he topped himself. Anyway, we'll just do our work, you know the way that we do? If we find an address book we'll let you know but these days that sort of thing's going to be on a computer isn't it, it's not the dark ages."

"I'm not trying to tell you how to do your jobs, truly, it's just that I've got a young woman missing. He could be involved; his mate almost certainly is. There is the chance that this might be murder, poison has been used before. I expect you could be right and he did this himself, taking into account the note and the bible, the empty pill packets, but I really, really need to know why and I need to know who he's been mixing with."

"Right."

Tanya was annoyed with herself, she needed to learn how not to wind people up. It had followed her through life, always in school getting on the wrong side of teachers, at the training college where she knew people called her a big head; antisocial. She was so used to having to hold her own, so used to fighting against being seen as the extra one, her sister the apple of her parents' eyes, the winner of all the prizes. It had made her forceful, it had been that or become a shadow, a follower, and she knew people saw her as prickly. Charlie had siblings, a crowd of them, but it had made him a team player, naturally sympathetic, a good reader of people. She had tried hard since she'd come back but she knew she had a tendency to come across as bossy, and you only got away with it when you were right, people were not as quick to be understanding when you screwed up, they liked to see you fail.

The door at the bottom of the stairs opened. "Charlie? Oh sorry. Inspector Miller." It was another person anonymised by the suit, hat, gloves. "We're in the garage. You probably want to see this." She grabbed the banister and ran down the stairs, "Come on Charlie, let's see if this'll tell us what the hell is going on here."

Chapter 38

It was cold in the garage; no sun could get in. Maybe in the middle of the summer with the door open but now, September, it was chilly. They had put a screen around the doorway. The road outside was busy with teens on bikes and boards, a couple of women stood hugging their jackets around themselves. Mrs Singh sat in the entrance to her flat; a little group of neighbours clustered together on the parking slab.

The work surface they had seen from their restricted view at the window was an old desk, it looked like something that had been used in an office at some time.

The boxes on the wall shelves were all similar, some white, some brown, all with labels on them. There were far more than had appeared from the outside, several hundred stacked neatly. On the desk were labels, lists, parcel tape, and a pair of scissors. Tanya shook her head, raised her eyebrows at the man who had brought them here.

"Well it's like a shipping office isn't it?" he said, as if it was obvious to anyone.

"How do you mean?"

In response he pulled open the flaps on the top of the nearest box. "Coffee in this one."

"Coffee?"

"Yeah, there's biscuits." He waved a hand towards the rear of the unit. "Tea bags, sugar, sauces in little tubes."

"Well, I don't understand. What, did he bulk buy?"

He gave a little laugh. "No, we didn't get it either, not until we started cataloguing the stuff. Look at the labels."

"I'm not into doing a quiz, can you just tell me what the hell this is all about?" She'd done it again, she tried a small laugh but it was too late.

He was taken aback by the snap in her voice, he had been amused by it all, until now, until he caught the atmosphere. She nodded, gave him a chance to carry on. "Well, okay. The labels on the boxes over there are all to the company who run the service area, not the big outlets, but the general place, the toilets and public spaces if you like. The drinks, the biscuits and so on are labelled for the motel. But those," he pointed to the shelves next to the desk, "those are all addressed to other places, same boxes, different labels. If you take a look at the book it's all pretty clear. Somebody has been nicking stuff from the services and running a nice little business selling it on."

Charlie's voice was muffled by the mask he was wearing but he nodded as he spoke, "Thou shalt not steal. That's the other well-known one isn't it? It wasn't about killing, the note, it was about bloody stealing stuff from work."

Tanya was shuffling papers on the desk, searching desperately for something with Peter's name on. "Is there a contacts list on this computer?"

"There's an order book there."

"No, not that, I don't know, a sort of staff list or something. Notes to a delivery driver?"

"Nothing I've seen but it's not really my job. We'll be taking the electronics away, giving it to the IT department."

"Look can we get this examined ASAP? I'm looking for reference to either a friend, or a colleague or, god I don't know. Anyway, somebody called Peter."

"Peter, oh right then, that'll be easy." With a grimace, the SOCO officer blew out a breath. "I'll see what I can do, we're short of people but I'll do my best."

"It's really urgent." Tanya pulled out her phone, opened the email to show him the artist's impression. "I have to find this bloke. I think he's abducted a young girl, if we don't get to her quickly, she's dead."

"We'll do what we can. Ping me your number, I'll ring you straight away if we find anything. We'll bag this up and get it shipped out."

"Can't somebody come here?" Tanya asked.

"Nope, can't do it that way. Got to have it opened under controlled conditions."

It was all they could do. They left the team to it. None of it was going to help, they hadn't expected a map and note telling them where to find Jane, or what was left of her, but they had for a while felt that they were getting somewhere. They were disappointed and disheartened.

"We'll go to the services, see if anyone there knows who this Peter is," Tanya said.

At the last moment, before they left, Tanya turned to the disgruntled SOCO officer, "Oh yes, and anything about angels, I need to know that as well."

"Angels?"

"Yes."

As they turned to go they heard him muttering under his breath, "Angels now, it'll be bloody Hobbits next."

Despite the circumstances Charlie couldn't hold back a grin.

* * *

The night manager was no help, he didn't know anything about someone called Peter, he hardly knew George Simpson, but made the point that he didn't like him. They rang the assistant manager Tanya had spoken to, but he was no help either. He was aware of Peter turning up now and then and having coffee with George Simpson, didn't think they were that friendly, but it was none of his business; again he made the point that he found George hard going, and hadn't been anything more than a work colleague.

They went through George's desk, his filing cabinet, everything appeared to be fairly straightforward, but now they knew it was not. He surely wouldn't have anything here that related to what they had found in his garage. They would have it all examined but they needed something quicker than going through staff lists that may well not exist, and delivery notes.

It was Charlie who mentioned the church. "If he helped with charity work, this Peter, then maybe the church would know who he was."

"Brilliant. But how do we find out which church? Do we know?"

"It's Methodist, we know that. I suppose we should start with the nearest one to where he lived."

Although it was late the pastor agreed to meet them at the church. "We have an office there. I think I know who you mean, but I don't have the information here at home. Is he alright? Is George okay?"

Tanya gave Charlie a thumbs up, they were already on the way, "I can't tell you very much at the moment, vicar, but I'd be really grateful for your help."

"I'm not a vicar, Inspector, but don't worry about that. I'll go and open up, see what I can find. Do you know where we are?"

"Yep, we've got you on the sat nav, thanks."

"Ah, marvellous isn't it?" With a chuckle he rang off.

Chapter 39

The church office was cold, Pastor Borthwick offered them coffee which they refused, trying to instil in him a sense of urgency. Again, he asked about George and they put him off, simply telling him that their enquiries were part of an ongoing investigation.

After what seemed an age, pulling out files, replacing them and moving on to the next battered old filing cabinet, he pulled out a plastic folder and placed it on the desk.

"I think it's in here. Peter Harper, that's who I had in mind. Do you think this could be who you mean? He did quite a lot of work with George, collecting things for the jumble," he shrugged, "all that sort of thing. He's had a hard life has Peter, his mother was an unfortunate I believe. Drugs and so on. Peter lived with his grandmother for a long time and then she had to be moved to a nursing home. If I remember correctly she died quite recently, a few months ago. His mother disappeared completely some years back. A bit of a loner I suppose you could say, but helpful." The pastor sucked at his teeth, lowered his head.

"Do you have a picture?"

"Not in here, these are just the general details of our helpers."

"Can we have those please?" She pulled out her phone ready to photograph the pages.

"Oh, I don't know. I mean what about erm, data protection and all that?"

"I promise you this is a matter of life and death, vicar."

"Not vicar."

"Okay – whatever. I could get a warrant, it would take time and I really need this information now. Please."

He stared at her for a moment, his brow furrowed, then turned back to the cabinets. "I think we might have a photograph here somewhere. Peter has some sort of minibus and sometimes helps out with transport. If you could be surer you see, if you could be more confident that he's who you mean." His voice was muffled as he bent over a low drawer. While he was looking away Tanya opened the file, took a picture of the page, and was betrayed by the flash in the dim room. The pastor straightened up, grabbing the file. He pulled it towards himself with a tut, replaced it with a parish magazine opened to a page about trips and visits. Tanya lifted the cheap little booklet to her face and peered at the small image accompanying the article. A bony finger pointed to a man in dark clothes at the end of the row of middle aged travellers. "That's him. Peter."

She turned on her phone torch, it was such a small picture, poor quality, it was too hard to see. "Can I take this with me?"

"Yes, of course."

"And the file?" As she spoke she grabbed the blue plastic folder.

"Oh, well that has other information in there."

She pulled it from his hand, "Give the pastor a receipt Charlie, I'm going to programme the sat nav." She knew she was wrong, that it could come back to bite them, but she was unable right then to be able to consider anything more than finding Peter Harper.

By the time Charlie joined her she had programmed in the address and was turning the car ready to pull out into the main road. The pastor stood by the little door watching them go, wringing his hands together and shaking his head.

"It'll be okay, Charlie. We'll find her and then it'll be okay." There was no response. She looked at his grim face, "I know that she's very probably dead, I get that, but what if she's not, what if she's somewhere scared and helpless and just waiting for us to come and get her? What if this Peter Harper has her, and for whatever reason she's still alive."

Charlie had picked up the parish magazine and was peering at it by the light of his torch. "It's too small this picture, I can't tell if he looks like the photofit, and I didn't see him in real life. God where's Sherlock with his magnifying glass when you need him?"

The robotic voice of the sat nav took them through Wheatly, across the A40.

Tanya's voice was quiet, "Kidlington, I haven't been to this place for a long time. It was where I saw my first body. Some poor druggie, left in a wood. We never did find out who she was." She sighed as she remembered the pale nightgown, the damage the rats had done, and the frustration that came from never knowing the whole truth. She pushed the musing aside, "This has got to be him, Charlie, it has to be."

Chapter 40

They were exhausted, they needed food and Tanya wanted a shower. She had pulled her hair back into its pony tail earlier and now her scalp felt sore and tight, she lifted a hand, pulled out the scrunchy and shook it loose.

Charlie leaned against the seatback and closed his eyes. She glanced at him, he had probably not had a full night's sleep since Joshua was born. She could see the tension and tiredness on his face. This job, this life asked so much, and the rewards were often hard to find. She saw his eyelids flicker, without moving his head he slanted his eyes at her, managed a smile. "Not asleep, honest, boss." She grinned back at him.

"I think we're nearly there, the sat nav says three minutes. So, it's not in the town, it's still pretty rural here."

Charlie sat up a bit straighter, yawned, "Sounds like a bit of an odd person, doesn't he? Of course it could just be because of his mum and that, but we have to have a look at least. Jane's got to be running out of time, assuming it's not already too late. It's the only decent lead we've had."

He thought for a minute before speaking again. "There was nothing at Simpson's place to indicate that he was involved. Once we found all that stuff in his garage we got the size of him: just a smarmy little pilferer – but there was nothing to suggest he was involved in this, was there?"

"There was the picture."

"What, this?" Charlie held up the church magazine.

"No, not that. Didn't you notice, in his lounge on the wall there was a picture. A print in a frame, a bit old fashioned."

Charlie was shaking his head.

"It was three angels. I didn't look at it closely, well we hadn't found him by then, but from what I remember it was three angels in a sort of woodland, all standing around, you know the way they do with their heads lowered and their hands crossed, all that malarkey."

"No, I didn't see that. Bloody hell."

She pulled onto the damp grass verge. "Okay I guess that's his place. It's bigger than I expected. A casual driver and odd job man, I thought he'd live in a little house, maybe a flat, but this is a bit grand."

"Well it's big, but it's ramshackle isn't it?" Charlie pointed to the long glasshouse, the moonlight glinting on shattered windows, roof struts like broken limbs against the grey sky. "The road's a wreck, the wall's down in places. Must cost a fortune to keep this sort of place up to scratch, but what can you do? Sell it in this state and you lose money, even if you can find a buyer. Anyway, he might not care. If it's been his home for a long time, perhaps he just lives here and doesn't think about it."

"Yeah. Let's walk down there, see if we can get an idea of what's what before he has the chance to tell us to bugger off."

They knew there were risks with this, anything they found would be inadmissible as evidence if they hadn't followed the rules. If they saw things that were suspicious they would have to gain entry legally, make sure all the 't's were crossed, apply for a warrant. Unless they found the missing woman, then they would be forgiven anything, maybe not by the legal systems but by their colleagues, and by themselves.

They closed the car doors softly. The road was loose gravel, crunching and scratching under their feet as they moved onto the verge. With the beams from the torches angled downward they stepped along the uneven ground. They kept the lights low, didn't want any chance that someone in the big square house, maybe looking out of the small panes of the upper windows, would see them before they wanted to be seen. Such stuff was what made watertight cases go pear-shaped, made rescue attempts fail. The unforeseen, the unlikely, it was impossible to prepare for everything, all you could do was your best.

They peered into the rear garden, the derelict greenhouse. There were a couple of other outbuildings, a garage, an old barn, two wooden sheds. Large deciduous trees cast moon shadows across the road, moving and shifting on roofs and lawns. The big barn had no door and they went in. It was almost empty, just a couple of sacks against a wall, an old bike in the corner and a pile of wooden fence posts. Charlie flicked his light upwards. Pigeons roosting in the dark became alarmed and fluttered; a couple flew through a hole in the roof, their wings clapping and whistling in the quiet.

Tanya whispered, "I can't see the van. If he still has it then it must be inside one of the other buildings, the doors are closed. We can't go in without a warrant." They walked around the garage, there wasn't even a window, the sheds looked dilapidated and rotten.

Charlie shook his head. "I don't think we're gaining anything. I reckon we might as well just go ahead and get him out of his bed, don't you?"

Tanya nodded. "Come on, let's get on with it."

They walked back to the gravelled path, up the shallow step and hammered on the front door. She glanced at her watch. It was past one in the morning. Was that late or early? Some people would still be up and watching television. She was already forming her response to the complaints that would probably follow this, if it did indeed turn out to be abortive. There was no light deep inside the house, they both knew that if Peter Harper was here he was in bed. She was committed now, she knocked again.

A light flicked on in the hallway, the glow spilling out through the fanlight above the front door. The locks rattled, the door opened a crack and then, suddenly, he pulled it wide and stood before them in a pair of boxer shorts, a grey T-shirt, his hair tousled, his eyes blurry with sleep. "What's the matter?"

It wasn't quite what they had expected, but hadn't they been told that he was a bit odd? They held up their identification. Tanya spoke, "Sorry to disturb you so late, Mr Harper. May we come in?"

"No." There was no enquiry from him about what they might want, just the simple refusal. So, either he was very aware of his right to refuse them entry, or he was being cautious, maybe difficult just for the sake of it.

She carried on, "We would like to ask you a few questions. I know it's late, but it is rather urgent, well very urgent. It's a bit cold." She lifted a hand, palm upwards.

"I'm not cold. What do you want?"

They had no other choice now but to try and question him on the dark doorstep. "We're looking into the disappearance of a young woman and we have reason to believe that you might be able to help us with our enquiries. We could go down to the police station or we could talk to you here which would be much quicker and easier."

He leaned forward, glanced back and forth across the yard. Turned his eyes back to where Tanya and Charlie stood on his step.

He stepped back and waved an arm in the direction of the hallway. "You'd better come in."

As he turned away, Charlie caught Tanya's eye. He nodded just once confirming what she had already decided. There was a definite likeness.

Chapter 41

As they walked along the hall, Peter turned on lights. It was chilly in the house. Dark wood furniture and heavy curtains looked as though they must have been there since the place was built. There were hooks along the wall, his jackets hung there and women's coats, old, with fur collars, velvet trim. There were hats, women's shoes, worn and dusty, an umbrella. She may be dead, but his grandmother still inhabited the house. There was no new furniture, nothing modern. It looked tidy enough but smelled stale – shut up. In need of sunshine and air. He showed them into a dark lounge. One small light hanging from a ceiling rose did little to brighten the place, the corners were shadowed and dim.

He was still wearing only his boxers and T-shirt. Charlie was the one who asked him if he wanted to put something else on, telling him that they would wait if he wanted to get a dressing gown. Peter shook his head and threw himself into an armchair beside the fire. There were no other sounds in the house, nothing to make them think there could be someone on the next floor. No reason to force their way up the dingy staircase.

"What is it you want from me?" His tone was less than friendly but couldn't be described as belligerent. It was a question, that was all. He didn't look at them, turning instead to stare at dead ashes in the fire. There hadn't been a blaze there recently, there was fallen soot from the chimney on top of the ash, some in the hearth. It wasn't a cosy home, the inside was a reflection of the parts they had seen on the exterior, shabby and going to seed.

Tanya pulled a picture of Sarah onto her phone, held it out towards him. "Do you know this woman?"

He glanced at the image and shook his head. She repeated it with another, one of Millie. His response was the same. Her final screen shot was of Jane, something her father had taken during the last week with him. She wasn't smiling, she looked a little irritated, a little embarrassed. He stared at this one a second or two longer. Tanya glanced at Charlie, raised her eyebrows.

"Doesn't look very happy, does she?" He handed back the phone with the quiet comment.

"You don't know any of these women?" Tanya asked.

He shook his head. "Do you have a car, Mr Harper?"

"I've got a van. I use it for work. I do gardening, a bit of delivering, house clearing."

"Do you use the M40?"

"Of course I do."

"When was the last time you were on the motorway?"

He wasn't defensive, didn't display much curiosity about the questions.

"Today."

"Do you ever go into the services?" Tanya said.

"Who doesn't?"

"Did you go to any of the service areas last week, on Friday for example? Friday evening specifically?"

"Can't remember. I might have done. I do deliveries, like I said. Maybe I did." He gave no indication that he had recognised Tanya from the brief time in Simpson's office. She decided not bring up that friendship yet.

They were getting nowhere, Tanya tried a different tack. "Would you have any objection to us having a look around?"

"A look around what?"

"Your house, your outbuilding. Could we see your van?"

"Now?" This was the first time that he had seemed at all disturbed.

"Yes, if you've no objection. It would help us to clear up a suggestion that has been made that you may be involved in the disappearance of these women." She wagged her phone at him.

"Who suggested that? Why do you think that?"

"Why? Because we have an image of a person we wish to speak to in connection with these issues and your name was given to us. I'm not willing to say who, of course, I imagine you knew that. I have to say that I do believe that there are many similarities in your appearance. Because of my suspicions I could request a warrant, it would take some time and when I came back I would bring my team with me to search your premises. Or, you could let us have a look around now."

He unfolded from his chair, pulled the T-shirt over his belly, and looked down at Tanya. "I want you to leave now. Go. I don't want to talk to you about these women. I've answered your questions, I don't have to do any more."

Without the documentation they had no option, he had asked them to leave and so they must. As he slammed the door behind them, plunging them into the gloom of the messy yard, Tanya turned on her torch and stepped onto the gravel. "I'm coming back. I'm coming back with a warrant and I'm going to tear this place apart."

She strode away down the narrow lane towards the car, paused just before she opened the door, pointed towards the dark shapes of trees in the distance. "It was over there, where we found that woman. The one that we never identified. Something grim about this area I reckon, Charlie."

Chapter 42

Tanya was quiet as they drove back through the quiet lanes. Charlie nodded off a couple of times, his head jerking backwards as he woke. He clambered from the car outside his house, dragged himself to the front door and disappeared without even a backward glance – too exhausted for niceties. It was well past four when Tanya walked into her own place.

Half an hour in the shower, surrounded by fragrant steam, the hot water pounding on her stiff shoulders and then she made coffee, strong and black. She knew she wouldn't sleep. Now that Peter Harper was alerted to their interest, Jane still out there somewhere, the thought of bed was impossible. There was something else though, something in the back of her mind that just wouldn't be dislodged. Harper was so like the image on the artist's mock up that she was almost ready to go to Bob Scunthorpe, but still vivid in her memory was the awkward conversation earlier about poor Kieran Laing. Would he think she was clutching at any tiny straw, flailing about for an answer, any answer to save face? It was torment.

She sat at the computer, read some of her emails. A pop up chimed on the screen, a favourite clothes site, a special offer on handbags. Automatically, she clicked through the images, put one of them into her basket. As she did it she felt a tingle in her gut. Something nudging at the edge of her mind, a shadow she couldn't quite see. Tony Stanley had tried to tell her about this. He'd told her about times when a case just wouldn't open up, it was tangled and unclear and then some tiny thing would start to niggle. She'd believed him, the evidence of his clear up rate was indisputable, he had been a hero not only to her but to plenty of others besides. She'd always known that the best of them, the sort that she aspired to be, had something else, some sort of sixth sense that showed them what others couldn't see. It set them apart, but she'd never really understood what he meant. Not until now, and it was so frustrating. She was dreadfully tired and yet still she couldn't switch off.

She stretched out on the sofa in the living room and closed her eyes. Then it began to unfold, she saw the hallway in that dingy old house, the clothes of a dead woman, the shoes, all seen in the dim glow of bulbs behind dirty shades.

She went back to the computer, brought up news reports, images of the great and the good, and the not so good. She skimmed the articles peered at the pictures. After a couple of hours, she had firmed up her thinking, convinced herself – almost.

Was it still too early to call Charlie? He'd been exhausted, absolutely out on his feet. It didn't matter, this was too urgent – there was plenty of time for sleep later. She dialled his number. She could hear the baby crying in the background. "Shit, Charlie is that my fault? Did I wake him up?"

"Nah, I have my phone on vibrate, he's had a bad night. Anyway, what's happening?"

She took a breath. "Listen Charlie, you know when we went in there…"

"Into the house?"

"Yeah, down that hallway with the coats and shoes. Well, did you notice anything that didn't fit, anything that struck you as out of place?"

There was silence for a while before he answered. "Nothing I can think of. What sort of thing do you mean?"

This was going to sound stupid, especially to a man. She almost told him that it was nothing, she'd been thinking out loud, but the niggle in her gut, the tiny growing shadow forced her to speak. "There was a handbag." There was silence, and it did sound a bit silly. She continued, "All the clutter in the hall was old, coats from years and years ago, shoes like ones my mum used to wear, tatty and old fashioned. There was a hook at the end, near the stairs, an umbrella was hanging on it, a shopping bag with some plastic carriers in and a handbag."

"Right." She could hear the puzzlement in his voice.

"It was modern. I've been researching it. It's only been available a few months, but here's the thing. It's really expensive, even I would hesitate to buy it. I found pictures of a few celebs, one of the younger royals, some wannabee film stars…" She paused, wondering if he would see; she wouldn't spell it out but let him come to it on his own – it would be more meaningful, more reassuring.

"Posh Spice or the Duchess of Cambridge! Sarah!" As he spoke she was swept with relief. She grinned. That was it, she'd been right. He was speaking again, "Was it that, do you think it was Sarah's bag, the one that she was struggling with?"

"We need to take a picture to Steven Blakely, I've printed a couple out. I'll pick you up in about half an hour."

* * *

Sarah's boyfriend looked haggard but holding it together. In the week since they had last seen him he had lost more weight, but he had an air of quiet about him, a sense of acceptance. He nodded silently when they showed him the picture of the bag. They had told him up front that it wasn't hers, that it didn't mean that they had caught her killer, it was just a lead they were chasing up. He handed the paper back to them, there was nothing else they could say, nothing they could give him to make him feel any better. It wasn't until they were in the car that Tanya allowed herself a smile.

Charlie asked, "So, back to Bob for a search warrant, we'll get the team up there." He glanced at his watch. "The idle buggers should have had their breakfast by now."

"I don't know." Tanya had pulled away from the kerb, heading back towards town. "I've been thinking about it, about Jane. If she has been fed the mushrooms, even if it wasn't right away, we know she's more than likely beyond help. I have to believe that there may be a chance that she has somehow avoided it. It's been a couple of days, that's all; maybe, just maybe she is still alive. If we take him in now, how do we find her? Do you think she's at the house? It seems unlikely to me, he asked us in too easily."

"Yes, but he wouldn't let us look around, wouldn't let us search the rest of it, wouldn't let us see his van. What are you thinking?"

"I want to get up there right now. Keep an eye on him at least. He might do something, now that we've disturbed him." She glanced across the car, "I should have done it right away, I've made a mistake I reckon, but it's still early. I want to get the team sorted and keep an eye on him. Let's see where he goes. I don't think there's much time. We have to do it now."

"We could go back, get in the house again, see if that handbag is still there. If it is then that's going to be plenty to bring him in."

"Yes, I know, but then what happens to Jane? By the time they've sorted out solicitors for him, gone through all the motions, then we've had a chance to question him, cope with delays for drinks, food, all the rest of it. Well, you know as well as I do that we'll lose hours. If we go and watch him now, maybe he'll lead us straight to her. Or, maybe if that doesn't happen at least he'll give us enough to drag him in and lean on him, get him really worried, and organise a search. My other concern is that now we've been, maybe he'll clean up his act. Maybe when we go back there, warranted up and all, the handbag will be gone, anything else will be gone; Jane, if she is there somewhere, will be gone, and we'll have played our hand." As she spoke Charlie registered that they weren't heading back to the office but towards Kidlington.

"Hang on. Drop me at headquarters. I'll get the team up to speed. We'll get down there within the hour. Don't go in there on your own. Wait for back up."

She nodded, her face grim, her knuckles white on the steering wheel.

Chapter 43

Tanya pulled the car into a turn off, and reversed carefully behind a hedge, watching out for soft ground. She mustn't bog down. Fortunately, there was only one reasonable way out of the group of buildings and the yard. If he had a four-wheel drive, an off-road trail bike, then of course he might go through fields. But she was alone. For now, she could only do what she could do. She pulled open her can of high energy drink. She hated these things, it would have her nerves popping and fizzing for hours but sitting in a quiet warm car in her exhausted state was the quickest way to miss something because she was asleep. She would never live it down, that sort of thing stuck with you.

It was too quiet, she felt her eyelids closing. High energy drink or not she was exhausted, she needed cold air, needed to move about. She pulled on her jacket and stepped out into the edge of the field, walked along the narrow road, close in against the hedge. As she came alongside the derelict glass house she clambered onto a piece of broken wall and peered over into the yard.

A dark blue people carrier was parked around the side of the house. It was old but clean. They had missed that in the dark the night before. On the side was an emblem, a shield with another shield inside, a couple of heraldic creatures, a bird, possibly a dove on the top. It was the wrong colour, pale against the dark blue of the van. It didn't have the words on the top that it should, but if you thought you were looking at a police vehicle, if you were a little confused or frightened, it could be convincing as an emblem for the force, provided you had just a glimpse and didn't know what to expect – if you were a young girl or a woman with other things on your mind. It looked like the emblem on the parish magazine.

The sun was up, and the morning was warming, birds flitted back and forth, a flock of pigeons wheeled and dived overhead. Other than that, it was quiet. Tanya guessed he was still there, hoped she hadn't messed up totally, allowing him time to flee.

She walked further along the track, behind the biggest of the outbuildings. They had been in there last night, there was nowhere for him to have hidden Jane Mackie. She stepped carefully along the tufty grass behind it. There were the sheds, ramshackle but not as badly decayed as they had seemed yesterday. She leaned towards the nearest, rubbed at the grimy window. There was no space in there to hide a woman, it was full of rubbish. She walked to the next, again it was just a wooden hut full of junk.

She turned back and retraced her steps. She would wait in the car for the others and then maybe explore a little further, unless he left the property. As she turned the corner at the end of the barn she stretched up on her toes, peered over the top of a wild hedge. A hundred metres or so distant, across a stretch of field, uncultivated and crowded with nettles and brambles, was another group of buildings. A small cottage, ancient by the look of it, with a front door of old unpainted wood and just two small windows, one on each side. The one on the right was boarded on the outside with planks. Beside that was a lean-to shelter with an ancient car rusting into oblivion inside. There was a storage place on the other side, no walls, just pillars holding up a sagging roof. Some ancient hay bales were stacked in there, dirty and discoloured, some of them broken, the stack tumbling towards the floor.

It could be part of the same property. There was no wall or fence between them, just this wild, rambling hedge.

She glanced back – no sign of life. She should wait. When Dan and Sue turned up she could leave one of them to watch for movement and they could walk over and have a look at this new location. She should go back to the car. She peered towards the house. The curtains in the downstairs rooms were still closed. It was before nine, Sunday, maybe he wasn't up yet. Did murderers have a lie in at the weekend? She didn't know.

The little cottage was calling to her, she'd have a quick look. If he started the car she'd hear it, she would have to wait for him to reach the junction anyway, before she could pull out of the field, otherwise he'd see her.

She set off across the waste land, ears alert for the sound of an engine.

The phone in her jacket vibrated. It was Charlie. "Sorry boss, it's about Sue and Dave."

"What?"

"There's been a huge smash on the motorway. It's closed, both directions."

"Tell them to use the hard shoulder, flash their badges."

"No, it's not on. They've gone as far as they can. The whole thing is a war zone. Nobody is getting through anywhere. They can't even get emergency vehicles through, they're bringing the Air Ambulance."

"Right. Who else is there?"

"Kate and Paul are at the services."

"What, why?"

"They're following up on the stuff with Simpson, do you remember?"

"Bugger. I'd forgotten that. Well they'll have to leave it. He's going nowhere and it's going to take ages to investigate all that palaver. There'll be quite a few others involved, got to be, but it's not urgent, not like this."

"Traffic have sealed the services. They don't want anyone else joining the cars on the road. Everyone is stuck. Can you hang on there? I'll come now, I'll use the back roads. Mind you everyone'll be using sat navs and they'll take all the traffic the same way, it's going to be mayhem, well it already is."

"Charlie, just do what you can. I meant to mention though." She paused, "This hasn't been approved, this surveillance. The overtime."

"Yes, we realise that, we're not daft. They're good with it."

This made her smile, in spite of the problems. Her team.

"I'll stay here and wait."

"Okay. Be careful though."

"He's still in bed, Charlie."

"Good, yes, that's good. I'll be with you as soon as."

She set off across the field, it was hard going, tangles of brambles grabbed at her legs, hidden rocks and holes threatened her ankles and more than once she was over her shoe tops in muddy puddles. She struggled on. If she had to run back because she heard Harper leaving she was in big trouble. Conviction pulled her forward.

Chapter 44

Tanya turned to look back at the house, nothing had changed: no lights, no movement. It had begun to drizzle with rain, she pulled up her hood and walked along the edge of the waste ground. The nearer she got to the cottage the more decrepit it looked.

The path at the front was damaged and overgrown, the garden no longer distinguishable from the surrounding land. There were a couple of rose bushes straggling round the door, but they hadn't been pruned in years.

The cottage, tumbling down and falling apart, had a new padlock on the front door. She lifted it, let it drop back against the wood. Nothing odd about that. It was probably still fairly weather proof, it would provide decent storage. Maybe it wasn't as bad as it looked, what did she know about property? There could be furniture inside, something worth securing.

She stepped onto the soggy ground beside the step and stretched up towards the window. The frame was rotten and one of the little panes was cracked. It was filthy of course. She took a tissue from her pocket and rubbed at the glass.

Light couldn't penetrate very far into this small house, but she could see a table, chairs, shelves. Dark corners. A pale figure moved in the grey, dim light. She gasped, jerked back with shock, gave a little snigger of embarrassment. *What the hell.* She leaned closer, her nose touching the pane.

Her stomach clenched. A wedding dress hung from a hook in the ceiling, swaying a little, surely in a draught allowed by ill-fitting doors and windows. It was ghostly and sinister but so much more than that, it was evidence.

Her nerves tingled and when the phone in her pocket vibrated her heart thumped with shock. She took a deep breath, pulled out the handset and pressed the answer button. Just another moment to get her breathing under control and then she spoke, "Charlie?"

"I'm at the end of the lane, where's your car?"

"I've backed into that gateway and then behind the hedge. There isn't room for two cars, can you find somewhere else?"

"Yes, if I go down the lane at the other side I can tuck in beside the wall. Do you want to come and sit with me or shall we have a two-pronged attack?" He laughed as he said it, remembering how she had been embarrassed by using the phrase with Bob.

"You stay there. I got out, moved around a bit, I was falling asleep. There's a building here, I've found something, it's important. We're going to be able to get inside his house now, no problem but I want to finish looking around here."

"What, what have you found?"

"I'll get back to you. Hang on there, try and get near to the glasshouse. I'll make my way to you in a few minutes."

She knew there was no point trying to take a picture through the filthy glass, the flash on her camera would obliterate everything but its own reflection. She had to get back, set things in motion. Bob Scunthorpe wouldn't refuse a search warrant now. She'd need it for the whole property.

Her phone vibrated again. Charlie.

She hissed at him, "I'm coming. Just hang on."

"No, listen. He's on the move. He's just left the house, front door, moving back now past the barns, northwards, on foot. He's carrying a holdall."

"Northwards! He's heading towards me. Okay. Look, I'll get behind these buildings if I can. Don't ring me. I need to watch, don't ring okay?" She glanced at the handset, she wasn't risking it ringing. She turned off the phone, stepped away from the cottage wall and sprinted to the barn, down behind the hay bales where she could see the front door. She could hear him now, he was coming.

She had been in tense situations before, many times, but never so much out on her own. It was fine, she'd be fine. She was just going to watch and then skirt the field back to Charlie and call in the troops. She crouched in the dusty, mouldy hay.

* * *

Peter Harper strode rapidly across the field, confident, determined.

He pushed a hand into his pocket and pulled out keys. He glanced around, not with suspicion so much as casual interest in the world around him.

To Tanya, he looked ordinary; he looked normal. Was he really a killer? Well, they didn't have horns, she knew that, they didn't have anything to set them apart, that was the most dangerous thing about them.

He put the small bag on the step. He needed two hands on the swollen door. He pushed it open, grabbed his holdall and disappeared inside.

Chapter 45

Jane tried to open her eyes, they were gritty and sore, the lids were heavy. Her mouth felt foul, gluey; her tongue too big for the space. She tried to swallow but there was no saliva. Her arms and legs were heavy, and her mind was sluggish and dull. It was cold, her bones ached. She moved, and the forgotten injury sent a screaming shaft of pain through her, and the throbbing started again. The reminder of her damaged foot brought it all back, the why and where, and she sobbed.

There was light in the splits and spaces of the roof, so it was day. What day? She had no idea. She heard the birds, the low whistle of the wind through a gap somewhere.

Every part of her body hurt, inside and out. She forced herself into a sort of wakefulness, pushed gingerly with her hands, holding the wounded limb away from the floor. She shuffled backwards, squealing and groaning, until she could lean against a beam, and sit almost upright.

The empty water bottle rolled away as she nudged it with her leg, the other one was still where she had put it, standing against the wall. She reached for it.

As she tipped it to her mouth she felt lukewarm liquid flood over her palm. She remembered. There was something wrong, something that had happened before. She licked the water from her hand.

It was the water that had made her ill, she had drunk the water and blacked out. It had to be the water. She lifted the bottle so that it caught what little light there was and saw the drip flash and glint as it fell. There was something in the water, pushed in through a hole in the plastic.

She wanted to drink so badly. She had been hungry for as long as she could remember now, through choice. She liked feeling hungry, feeling hungry meant a negative calorie balance, meant that all the ugly fat was melting away. But she hated being thirsty. She needed water. But the water had been bad.

She tipped the bottle, licked the spills from her hand again. It didn't taste bad, didn't taste of anything but water.

She lifted the neck of the bottle to her lips, sipped, waited. Nothing happened, she sipped again. Her body was crying out for the liquid. She felt thirstier now than she had before she had begun to sip. It hadn't been enough to swallow properly, just enough to wet her mouth. She drank again, a bigger mouthful. She swallowed. Nothing happened.

She held the bottle away from her, looked at the empty one on the floor. She had drunk it, she had been drugged, she must have been. That was the only thing that made any sense. Her foot throbbed, her body ached, she was cold, alone and afraid.

While she had been asleep she hadn't been any of those things, yet now that she was awake it had all started again.

She looked around the dingy place, listened to the wind in the rafters, the birds in the gutter. Tears filled her eyes. Where did tears come from when your body was so dehydrated? She wiped them away.

While she was asleep there had been no fear, no pain, no tears.

She lifted the bottle to her lips and swallowed several mouthfuls. She laid her head back against the rough wall. After a short while the room spun, just a little; she felt nauseous. The pain in her foot receded.

She picked up the bottle, emptied it in a few gulps, slid back down on the floor, laid on her side, closed her eyes and fell back into the darkness.

* * *

Downstairs the door creaked open. Peter Harper stepped inside, through to the kitchen at the back of the cottage. He glanced around, looking at his pictures – the walls were lined with angels. They weren't all his, some of them were from the internet, some of them were from magazines and books but they were all perfect.

The girl upstairs wasn't perfect, she was ruined. He couldn't fix her, couldn't use her. He couldn't make a broken girl into an angel. Mum hadn't been perfect, not at first. Granny had explained it when he was little, how it was so much better for them if Mum became an angel. Then they didn't need to worry about her anymore.

Granny made sure he went to school, taught him about all the things she knew: how to keep chickens, how to kill them quickly. How to forage, about the mushrooms; she had made sure he knew which ones were safe.

She told him about the drugs his mother had taken, the things that had turned her bad. But they weren't dangerous if you knew what you were doing and she taught him about that. She made sure he'd be okay when she was gone. She had left him money, the house – all he'd need. She had been his best friend, reading together, watching her favourite programmes: the police ones, the church ones on Sundays.

He had worked this bit out for himself though: the way to make perfect angels, no wrinkles like mum had, beautiful golden hair, just like the ones in his pictures, just like his mother had been after they had changed her. These women, angry and upset when he saw them, they were so much better once he'd turned them into angels.

He took out the things that he had brought, he laid them on the table. She might still be asleep, he had put plenty of the drug into the water. If she had drunk it all she would still be asleep, she may even be dead already. That would be best, if she was dead already he wouldn't have to do anything else.

He took down the picture of his mother, granny had taken it for him. She was so pretty. Not the other woman, the drunkard, the screaming harridan who had struck him and pushed him, called him names, and burned him with her cigarettes. This was his real mother, an angel. Like the other women, ordinary until death had made them special. He always knew which ones they were, he just had to look at them. They were slender, tall; their hair, long and pale – pale like their skin, like the picture. Angels walking on earth, but angry because they shouldn't really be here.

He left the kitchen and went to look at the gown. He lifted it and let the fine fabric float back in the little draught from the open door. It was beautiful. He needed another woman the same size as the one upstairs. She would have been just right, maybe a little short, but that didn't matter. He would need to find another one the same; they had to fit – that was very important. She was so thin though, like a reed. He had to find someone just the same. He could get another dress, it was easy. They didn't notice in the shops but this one was lovely. He'd found it in the jumble, that was a shame. He'd even washed it, very carefully; it had been muddy, and now it would be a waste if he couldn't use it.

First, he must take care of the reject. He should have known that she wasn't right. She had fought him. The others just came, they weren't afraid, they had gone to sleep beautifully in his van and then they had eaten the soup when he promised they could go home afterwards. They had gone home; he had sent them home. This one had been wrong from the start. She was a mistake, so it didn't matter where he put her. He might just leave her here for a while. He could use the downstairs bedroom again for the next one. Nobody ever came, and it was difficult climbing up the ladder anyway. Yes, he'd leave her here. He'd brought some bin bags. If he sealed them up he knew it wouldn't smell. When they killed all the chickens because of the bird flu, they'd done that and then got rid of them later, when there was nobody looking. He'd put what was left out in the woods, in the place Granny had showed him, far away from the paths. The wild animals would take care of it, and that would be that.

Chapter 46

Tanya watched him go in and moved towards the corner of the cottage. She took another few steps towards the window, bending low, just enough to see over the edge. He wasn't in the room at the front, but she could hear him. She crept to the opened door. There was another room at the end of the hallway. He had opened the back door to let in light. She could see there were papers on the wall, the breeze from the door made them waft and crackle.

He was out of sight. She walked around the corner, slid into the house. Tight against the wall she moved along the hallway and into the room on the left of the door. She could see a glimpse of him now and then moving in the kitchen, by the old sink and the ancient gas cooker.

Nobody lived here. It was damp and cold and filthy. She looked at this room. It was bare, no carpet, no furniture. There was a door in the corner furthest from the window. With quiet steps she crossed the floor. It was a bathroom, there was a cracked and stained porcelain bath, a toilet and a wash basin, the tap dripping onto a brown stain. There was a heap of dark fabric in the corner. She glanced back, listened, he was still in the kitchen.

When she picked up the clothes she knew immediately what they were, had to stifle a gasp at the evidence in her hands. She had been a fool. She had no gloves on and here she was handling the top that Millie had worn in the picture taken at the airport at the end of her holiday. She dropped it back onto the pile.

Harper was walking back towards the other room, she watched as he lifted the hem of the awful wedding dress, let it fall, and ran his fingers down the length of the skirt.

She dodged back as he turned to the door and again plodded towards the kitchen carrying his bag.

The ladder from a trap door rattled and crashed, loud in the quiet house. He lifted the hold all and hefted it up before him, pushing it towards the ceiling and into the loft. She watched from her hiding place as his body and then his legs disappeared into the dark space in the roof.

Dust shuttered down into the hall from the ceiling plaster as he moved about. She heard him talking. There was no answer.

It must be Jane, it had to be. It didn't matter, if it wasn't Jane then whoever it was shouldn't be there in the gloom of the roof. There could be no good explanation for that, not even an animal should be kept there.

She went to the ladder and climbed onto the first rung. Now she could make out some of the words. There was no answer, just his muttering – reassuring, calming.

She climbed the ladder, poked her head above the trap. There she was, the pathetically small shape curled against the edge of the roof, the great bulk of Peter Harper bending over her, the scene lit by a single bulb high up in the rafters.

She caught the shine of polythene as he shook out the bag, heard the rustle as he gathered it in his fists.

He knelt beside the unconscious girl, still speaking softly, telling her it wouldn't take long, that she would feel no pain, telling her he was sorry, but she was too broken to be an angel.

He rested her head on his kneeling lap, raised his hands, the bag gripped between them, and pulled it over the tangle of her long blond hair. He dragged it down over her brow. It caught on her nose but briefly. It was calm, unhurried; Jane made no protest, no effort to resist.

Tanya screamed, "Police, stop!" she hoisted herself from the ladder, scrabbling with arms and legs into the roof space.

He turned to her, his face shocked, and drew away. Jane's head slid from his knees as he scuttled backwards. The inert form didn't move, didn't react as her skull thudded onto the boards. Tanya glanced at her, the bag covered half her face but still her mouth was clear.

He was standing now, confined by the slant of the roof, bent almost double but coming towards her, his hands reaching in front of him. Fast and heavy and alarmed, propelled by shock and anger.

She turned aside, back towards the hatch, but he caught at her, pulled her in towards him with one strong arm, the other steadying himself against the low wall.

He fell, dragging her on top of him, on her back, her shoulders straining forward. She kicked and squirmed in his arms, twisted, and then jolted backwards with her head with all the power she could muster from her confined position. She felt his nose shatter, saw stars herself, and cried out at the stab of pain.

One arm loosened as he grabbed at his face. She rolled, freed a hand, pulling and clutching at his other arm, but already he had her again. This time when she thrust back with her skull he dodged, she hit the side of his face, a glancing blow – useless.

He rolled now, turning her with him, had her pinned under him, sitting astride her, the great bulk of him squeezing the breath from her lungs; she gasped, tried to draw in air. He moved his hands to her neck – gardener's fingers, strong, hard, around her throat. Squeezing, tighter, tighter.

Lights flashed behind her eyes. She heard a whistle, high and piercing; deep inside her skull, darkness gathered. The roof, the man, the panic, began to recede – peace was waiting. She kicked her legs on the boards, she couldn't feel her hands, she couldn't see, there was nothing any more; it was all gone.

Chapter 47

Tanya was aware of rough hands, something pulling at her. Her neck hurt, her throat was on fire. Her body had taken over and dragged air into her lungs as soon as the restriction had moved. Her chest hurt, heart pounded and there was thunder in her brain.

"Tanya, come on, breathe, keep breathing. Christ, come on."

"Charlie." She pushed at him, shook her head, tried to move away from him.

"Sit up, come on."

"Jane?"

"I've got the bag off, she's breathing. She's completely out of it, but she's breathing at least."

"Harper?" With oxygen in her lungs and her heart steadying, she felt strength returning quickly. She raised a hand to her bruised and reddened neck. "Shit, that's sore."

"I'm not surprised, it's black and blue already."

"What happened?"

"I tried ringing you, went to voicemail and I didn't like it at all. I waited but he was gone too long."

As he spoke she realised just what it meant. "Thanks Charlie."

He nodded. "There's an ambulance on the way. God knows how they'll get here, the motorway is still a mess but anyway, I've called them."

She crawled to where Jane lay, Charlie's jacket covering her shoulders. "Where is he?"

"He ran. I couldn't do much about it. I was more concerned right then with you – with her." He pointed to the girl. "I've put out details of the van and what have you. He can't get far, we'll find him." At this point he touched a finger to his face, she noticed the swelling beneath his eye, the smear of blood on his lip.

"You fought him then?"

"Dragged him off more like, just pulled him away. He clocked me one and then practically fell down the ladder. I couldn't follow, I didn't know whether you were okay or…" He trailed off, they left the rest of it unsaid.

"Do you think we should move her downstairs?" She was stroking the hair back from Jane's forehead as she spoke.

"No real point I don't think. It's no better down there and when the paramedics get here they'll be more skilled at it than we are, best leave her."

Tanya peered around the loft. "There are clothes downstairs, in the room on the left, I reckon they belonged to Millie. There's a wedding dress, hanging in the other room. Really spooky that."

"Yes, I saw that and the pictures."

"Pictures?"

"I didn't get much more than a glance while I was trying to find you. They look like pictures of angels. All over the walls in the kitchen."

"Oh, is that what they are? I saw there was something."

"Yeah, it's covered with them. We've found him. Not much doubt about that."

"We have, but we haven't got him, have we? He's still out there."

"True, but he's not going to do it again, is he? Not now he knows we're onto him."

Tanya shook her head, "I don't know Charlie. He's off his chump isn't he. How can we know what he might do?"

"We'll have him by the end of the day. Got to."

"I bloody hope so."

They heard the sirens in the distance, Tanya breathed a sigh of relief. "You stay with her, I'll go and meet them." As Charlie stood, his head and shoulders hunched in the low room, Tanya held out a hand.

"Thanks Charlie." He simply shook his head and turned away. Her eyes filled with tears. She sniffed, it was just a result of the shock, that was all. She bent and tucked his jacket tighter around Jane's skinny shoulders.

There was no sign that the girl had been vomiting, all there was in the loft were empty water bottles, a bucket in the corner with a tiny amount of what must be urine in the bottom. Had they saved her? She was here, she was breathing, but was she doomed? They would have to wait to find out but for now it was enough that they had found her.

It was a difficult job to bring her down. They put her on a back board with a collar around her neck. They had no idea what injuries she might have so they had to take all the precautions. Once they had manoeuvred it through the hatch though, the stretcher slid down the wooden ladder and they were able to finish setting up the infusion to rehydrate her. Tanya told them about the poison, but there was nothing they could do until they had her at the hospital. They alerted the accident and emergency to the possibility, but even as they did it they all knew that it was a lost cause if she had indeed been fed the mushrooms.

Tanya refused the offer to take her in for a check over. "I'm fine, really." They gave her a couple of paracetamol to help with her pain and recommended she have someone check her over as soon as possible. "There could be damage to your throat, you need to get it looked at."

"I will, I will. But later. For now, we still have to find this bastard."

Chapter 48

Sitting in Bob Scunthorpe's office, him in his golf clothes, the officers outside in weekend mode, Tanya refused coffee but accepted a bottle of chilled water. It was bliss sliding down her sore throat.

"Are you sure you don't need the hospital?"

She wished people would stop asking her that. Okay it looked horrible and it felt awful, but it was just something that had to heal, it wasn't important. She shook her head, managing a thin smile.

"Have you any news about Jane Mackie?"

Now she was able to grin broadly, she had been looking forward to this. "Yes, she's very dehydrated, she has a really nasty injury to her foot, which they'll need to operate on when she's strong enough but..." She took a breath, enjoyed the moment, "there's no sign of poisoning. They've been able to talk to her and she says she didn't eat anything, only drank the water. It's crazy but it looks as though being anorexic saved her. Now that they have her they can try and address that as well. The poor thing has been to hell and back, but she'll get proper care now and she's young. With luck and plenty of support she'll be okay. Kate is there with her. She's weak and doesn't know all that much more than we already do. Still she'll be going home, eventually."

"That is really great news." He stopped, moved the pen on his blotter. "Peter Harper?"

Tanya shook her head. "Nothing yet, sir. We've got all units aware, the rest of my team are out there. We have crime scene investigators at the cottage. They've found jars of dried mushrooms, other drugs which have gone to the lab. There were bottles of bleach. The van is missing of course but we have plenty of evidence against him. It looks as though he kept Sarah in his own house and then moved on to the cottage with Millie and Jane."

"We need to find him, Tanya, we need to be able to show that we found him."

"Yes sir."

"Have you any news about that other business? The theft and the suicide."

She was able to tell him that Kate and Paul had found three more suspects they believed had been involved. "What is interesting is that they are pointing towards Harper with that."

The Chief Inspector raised his eyebrows. "How so?"

"Deliveries. It sort of makes sense. He knew just where to park to avoid the cameras, was very familiar with the back ways in and out of the services. He told us himself that he did deliveries. It does also make a bit of sense of what seemed like an overreaction by Simpson. He must have had an idea that Harper could be involved with snatching the women. He must have picked up on the fact that he was strange. Possibly the timings fit. That might have been the guilt he was feeling rather than simply the pilfering and the glitches in his past. We'll know more when we find Harper."

"Right. So, I think you should go home, Tanya. Get some rest. You've done what you can for now. The team are out there, take tonight to recover."

She argued, wanted to be out with the rest of them but in the end, tiredness, soreness and Bob's insistence wore her down. She went to the office where Charlie was filling out paperwork before heading out to join the others.

"I'll see you in the morning, Charlie. Ring me if there's anything, anything at all and no matter what time, yeah?"

* * *

The flat was warm and welcoming. She took a shower, pulled on her soft pyjamas and crawled under the duvet. She didn't think that she would sleep and for a while the recent events played and re-played in her mind, but she hadn't been to bed for more than twenty-four hours and she fell into a deep sleep.

It was dark when she woke, pitch black outside and it was quiet. She felt much better, though swallowing was still difficult.

Down in the kitchen with a bottle of fridge cold water in her hand she stood by the window staring out at the night. He was out there, he surely wasn't a danger anymore, they had found him, they knew who he was, and he had to be afraid, on the run. It was just a question of time. By now his bank accounts would be frozen, cards cancelled and if the number plate on the van was picked up by the cameras they would have him. However, he was crafty – far from stupid, even if he was deranged. He probably knew to keep away from the motorways, town centres. Where would he go? She frowned and chewed at her lower lip. Where would he hide?

She sat at her desk making notes, letting ideas come. She pulled up the reports that had been forwarded on, the pictures of the interior of the house. She clicked through them: the attic, the front room and pile of clothes, the dreadful wedding dress which had been intended to be a shroud for Jane. Then she saw it among the pictures on the wall of the kitchen. The slender figure in a pale gown, posed in the woods. No evidence of damage, no tiny teeth marks, no soaking turning the white nightdress to grey.

She wrote an email to the forensic section, told them where to look for the records. They had DNA, all they needed now was him, and then they could put a name to the corpse in the rain. The first of his angels.

They were putting his picture on all the news bulletins, so his friends, if he had any, must be aware of the situation. He couldn't turn to them.

Where would *she* go? She kept herself to herself, didn't bother with her sister. The only people she really interacted with were work colleagues, and Peter Harper worked alone. Deliveries, gardening. She must arrange tomorrow to visit anywhere he did that. House clearance he had said. She glanced at her watch. It was just after three in the morning. She was refreshed and wide awake. She stuck a couple of slices of bread into the toaster and then realised toast was not really an option. She'd have yoghurt. She turned on the coffee maker and ran up to her room for some clothes.

His computer was in the office, they had been working on it and probably it was too soon to expect a report, but it must be there, in the headquarters. She had no choice but to wait for morning. She swallowed some yoghurt, drank coffee cooled to acceptable with lots of milk. By five she was dressed and ready, her fingers tapping at the keyboard, trying to be patient. She needed to move now, she couldn't let him get away. This was nearly over, nearly a success; despite the two women victims it had gone well, though they would always haunt her. She accepted that, it was part of the job. They had that right.

Chapter 49

The IT department worked on a flexible time system, and the first computer nerd turned up at seven. Tanya was standing in the corridor, leaning against the wall, scrolling through messages on her phone, catching up with reports from the day before.

He sighed when he saw her, he'd been planning on a nice relaxed coffee before anyone else came in. Anyway, he booted up his machine and inserted the drive they had made as a clone of Harper's computer. She signed the requests, formalised everything, pleaded with him to let her have hard copies of the diary entries, the casual database of work that he had. There would be stuff here, hidden somehow, but to do with the delivery of stolen goods; she'd pass that on to Kate to work through but what she wanted was his customer database. His records of house clearances. As the printer spat them out she grinned her thanks at the technician and jogged up to her own office.

There weren't that many. She shouldn't do this on her own. She could call Charlie or one of the others, but they had finished late last night, and this was just an idea. It could come to nothing.

She opened Google Maps, put in the first address, printed out a copy of the map and then used an old-fashioned pen to mark the other places. It didn't seem that he travelled far, he used the council tip often and of course the charity shops. He had them marked with the name of the manager and whether they sold wedding dresses. She smiled as another little key slotted home.

The first two addresses were small houses, terraced and occupied. Either the residents who had employed his services had been having a clear out or, if they had been sold, they already had new owners. The third was a flat in the top of a block of expensive apartments, speaker entry systems, heavy duty locks on the front and back doors. No way.

Then her route took her away from the city of Oxford, out into the countryside. A small village with a big name: Woodstock. Famous for Blenheim Palace but small in terms of a town. The address was in a narrow street of stone houses. She parked in the car park by the library, even this early it was nearly full, but the on-street restrictions gave her little choice. She walked through the winding streets. The houses had bay windows with tiny panes, old doors with fanlights. It was very English, quaint. The house that he had cleared had scaffolding erected over the three-storey frontage. The lower windows were protected with boards. There was a small gate that gave entry to a side passage. It was old and mouldy with iron nail heads in the panels, and a rusted old handle. She reached out and was surprised when it opened.

She pushed into the narrow passage and closed the gate behind her. It was damp, weedy and neglected and led to a tiny rear courtyard garden. There was no sign of life.

Tins of paint, planks of wood and other building debris had been dumped in what should have been a charming little space. A set of furniture covered in plastic sheets was piled in a corner, forlorn and dirty.

The rear windows were boarded the same as the front, protection from the machinations of builders. She walked to the door, bent low to look at the doorknob. There were scratches here, grooves in the wood, damage that was not in-keeping with the degree of protection elsewhere. This was probably a listed building, had to be treated with respect, not dug at, and besmirched with a careless screwdriver.

She stepped back. She should call for back up. Charlie would be awake now, Joshua would have seen to that, surely. But, if she was wrong, it was a long way for him to come on a wild goose chase and there was plenty of other stuff for him to be getting on with.

* * *

The floor inside was gritty and covered in sheets of polythene. The smell was damp plaster, paint and putty – an old-fashioned smell in an ancient house. The small square kitchen had been stripped of units and the tap dripped into a plastic bucket standing on black and white tiles.

She paused, listened. There was nothing. But that back door should have been secured, the garden gate fastened.

There was a narrow hallway, a flight of stairs to the upper floors and doors into rooms at the front. She glanced into them and found more of the same: polythene, paint cans, folding work benches. On the stairs, in the dust, there was just one set of footprints, heading upwards. Big, man-sized. She took in a breath, pulled the can of PAVA spray from her shoulder bag and began to climb.

Chapter 50

The boards on the windows let in little stripes of light, enough to walk around without her torch. She glanced into the bathroom, a nasty sixties suite was in here, the green plastic bath was the same as her mum and dad used to have. There was a room at the front, empty, dirty and one at the rear overlooking the little garden. She turned on the half landing and went up to the next floor. The rooms there were not as big, having sloping ceilings, and smaller windows. They hadn't got this far with the boarding and it was easy to see that the rooms were empty. So, it had been a wasted journey. She was glad now that she hadn't bothered anyone else. The landing on the third floor was a small square, there was a trap door above it and she wondered for a moment, remembering where she had found Jane, but it would be a squeeze for her to get through and Harper was much bigger than she was. The only other door was beside the tiny second bathroom, in the centre of the house. It was a linen closet. Instinct told her to check everywhere.

He didn't give her a chance to pull the door fully open. As soon as it had moved a crack he burst forward. The door smashed into the side of Tanya's head, knocking her towards the steep staircase. She spun and clung to the newel post at the top, her ears ringing, tears of pain blurring her eyes. He strode towards her, two steps only for his long legs in the small space. She had regained her balance, planted her feet more firmly on the creaking boards but he was on her now. Grabbing and clawing at his face she tried to drive him backwards. She screamed at him. The blow from the door had knocked the spray can from her grasp and it had rolled into the corner, out of reach.

She was lifted bodily, yelling, and twisting in his arms. He moved half a pace sideways to the top of the stairs, tensed, leaned, and hoisted her above the level of the balustrade.

She clutched at his sweatshirt, grabbing the edge of the hood, the tie string tangling around her fingers. She kicked at him, tried to aim her foot at his groin, but couldn't get the space, the angle was all wrong. She tried to headbutt him, but he pulled back. Now she had squirmed sideways and hooked her feet around the banister rails, wrapping her arms more tightly around his neck. She tried to bite, to claw, but he bent and leaned and jerked away.

Then he dragged her forward, forcing her feet from the rails. She shouted with the pain in her ankles, she thumped and hammered at him – any part of him that she could reach. He was strong, but she was fighting for her life and desperation made her more than she was.

She stretched up, pulled his head forward, bending him at the waist, her fingers locked in his hair. She opened her mouth and clamped her teeth onto his cheek. He screamed, his arms loosened, she fell, thrusting him away, grabbing again at the banisters as the force pushed her backwards down the first two steps.

He had covered his face with his hands, blood was seeping between his fingers. He wiped at the bloodied cheek, looked down at her, shook his head, turned and ran from the tiny landing into the bedroom at the front of the house. She was after him before he had a chance to slam the door.

He lurched across the boards and launched himself at the window, smashing through frame and glass and landing in a heap on the scaffolding in front of the house. He rolled onto the wooden walkway. One of the vertical metal poles stopped his forward movement but momentum carried his legs over the edge. He began to slide. Though she didn't know what his intention had been, she watched in horror as instinct caused his hands to clutch at the metal bars. Gravity pulled him further, his legs kicking and flailing in mid-air.

It was too far for her to reach him from inside. She would have to step onto the scaffolding. It shuddered with the weight of him dangling two floors above the street.

He raised his face to look at her, blood from the bite wound dripping from his chin, fear widening his eyes, bruised black from where she had broken his nose in the cottage. She felt the ache in her ankles, remembered the pathetic curled heap of Jane in the attic, the sparkle and gleam of beads and sequins on the gowns of his angels. She knew that he was mad, that the legal system would put him in a place of safety. Sarah wasn't coming back, Millie wasn't coming home. There was no justice for them, nothing could change their fate.

She heard the screech of car tyres in the street outside, the shouts of pedestrians gathered to look up at the man hanging from the scaffolding.

His blood slick hands were slipping on the metal pole, he was sliding downwards, away from her, out of her reach.

Chapter 51

Sirens screamed in the distance. Someone in the street
below had stopped filming long enough to do some good
and call the emergency services. The sound of colleagues
racing towards her snatched her back to the present, to the
thing she had to do. Tanya stepped through the window –
clinging to the frame, and crouching – out onto the
scaffolding. Her stomach lurched when she saw the
distance from the ground, the upturned faces in the street
below. She pushed back the panic and focused on the man
in front of her, sliding further over the edge. The fingers
of one hand clawed around the pole. His legs flailed less
wildly, his attention was on his upper body. She saw the
desperate grip, the bulging muscles of his arms that were
beginning to quiver and shake. She reached for him,
wrapped a hand around one of his wrists. His other hand
was clinging to the edge of the walkway where a metal
strut ran under the wood, an inadequate grip. This arm was
further away, a different angle, harder to reach. She forced
herself to let go of the window frame, moved a few inches,
nearer to the edge. The crowd were mostly quiet,
suspended in the drama. Now and then when Harper's
legs moved, or the scaffolding groaned and creaked,

someone would scream, and there would be a communal gasp.

His wrists were thick, Tanya's hands didn't wrap all the way around, there was no way she could drag him back to safety, the most that she could hope for was to hold him until help arrived or he found his own way to clamber back. She was exposed out here, kneeling on the rough boards, nothing to cling to if he fell, as surely he must. He would drag her with him and they would both plummet into the street below. She should lay across the boards, hook her feet around the window frame. She didn't know how to do it, couldn't find a way. Her legs were tucked under her body in a half crouch. She had made a terrible mistake. She needed to stretch her legs out from beneath her, she couldn't force her body to obey. Terrified to move in case that was the moment he lost his battle with gravity, she was frozen.

His eyes met hers, terror reflected in them. "Come on." She managed a gasp, "Come on you bastard." She stretched further, slid her hand around his wrist a little tighter, further up his right arm. She bent her upper body nearer to the boards, if she could just stretch out her legs she would be safer, she needed to do it now. She glared at him, "Come on."

She saw as his eyes shut down, watched as he accepted what had become inevitable; she felt his hand relax, saw the fingers loosen. She would go with him when he went, he knew that didn't he? She saw that he knew that.

She wasn't ready to die.

She let go her grip, closed her eyes and listened to the screams.

The thud of his body was faint where she was but after a second of shocked suspension, the crowd erupted in turmoil.

* * *

There were things she should do, she ought to take charge but for now, with her knees turned to water and her heart pounding, all she was capable of was falling back onto her behind and leaning against the window frame. She knew already that his face, as he gave up the struggle, would stick with her for a long time, maybe forever.

She had tried. She had tried as hard as she could. Hadn't she? Had the few moments that she hesitated, her mind filled with thoughts of the dead women, made that much difference? Had fear for her own safety caused her to fail? She lowered her head onto her knees and let the shock and reaction have its way.

As soon as she was able she gathered herself and, with a deep breath, swivelled around, jumped back into the room, and went to join the first responders who had screamed to a halt outside, sirens wailing, blue lights bouncing reflections from the windows of the houses in the narrow street.

As she brushed the tears from her face and crossed the room towards the stairs she pulled out her phone and called Charlie.

"I'm in Woodstock. Can you come?"

She told him only that she'd found Harper, there'd been an incident, gave him the name of the street and assured him that he'd find it, no problem, and it would be best if he came over as soon as he could. Dragging out her warrant card she stepped into the crowded scene, glancing just once at the broken body on the flags. She didn't need more, she had witnessed his last moments, it was enough. Incredibly none of the gawping bystanders had been hurt, though one or two were sitting on the pavement quaking with shock, tended by friends or strangers. The officers from the cars were pushing back those who still wanted more of the spectacle and the paramedics knelt beside Peter Harper, no infusions, no attempt at resuscitation, their quiet told her everything there was to know.

* * *

By the time Charlie arrived they had a plastic cover shielding Peter Harper's corpse. The road was closed to all but the police vehicles. Tanya was back inside the house, sitting on an upturned box sipping a cup of strong tea stolen by a policewoman from the provisions the builders had kept in a carton in the kitchen.

She heard Charlie's voice outside, put the thick paint-spattered mug on the floor and went out to where he was catching up on what had happened.

"Hiya Charlie."

"You okay, boss?"

She nodded at him, managing a smile. "I don't know why I called you, Charlie. I don't know what you can do really. We're waiting for the van to take him away. There's no mystery here, I was part of it, but I just wanted some support." She knew she sounded weaker than she should. If it had been anyone else she couldn't have been so honest, but this was Charlie. He raised a hand, she knew his instinct was to hug her, that was how he was, but he touched her shoulder just once, nodded, looked up at the broken window, "I thought you didn't like heights?"

"Yeah well, nothing's changed there." She hoisted her bag onto her shoulder. "I'm in the car park, I'll meet you at the end of the road. Best get back, there'll be a heap of paperwork after this and I could murder for a bacon sandwich."

"Good enough, and I think it's your turn for breakfast. All the team'll be there. This is going to cost you."

With a last glance at the plastic tent she turned away. There was still a lot to do.

Chapter 52

The team were hyped up. There was a round of applause as Tanya and Charlie walked into the office, their hands full of bags from the café. She grinned at them. That was nice. The drive back to Oxford and the bacon sandwich had done a lot to calm her nerves.

There would be off-colour jokes, black humour, and despite the little knot of horror deep inside she knew that she would laugh and shake her head and let them believe she could shrug it off and leave the experience behind her.

There was a meeting later with the boss, there was the paperwork, the internal enquiry; it would all move on.

She would go to the funerals, both of them, they would send flowers from the team. No court case though, not this time and it was a sort of blessing because they all knew that he hadn't been fit to be tried and it would never have felt enough seeing him locked away in a secure hospital.

She would go to the other grave as well, just take some flowers. Now that there was a name, she could write it on the label – recognition.

"So, I need to get up to speed on the pilfering. What's the situation there?"

Charlie shrugged. "Kate and Paul have got it pretty much wrapped up I reckon. There were four other people involved, three from the hotel and one from his office, a secretary. She had a hand in fiddling the books. I don't think they were making much from it to be honest, it's all a bit low key, a bit sordid. But it's another point for us, isn't it?"

"I wonder whether he killed himself because of the theft or more because he had an idea that Peter Harper was – well who he was."

"Apparently he'd been part of the congregation at the church Simpson preached at most often. People there said that they were close. He might well have had an idea that there was something not right about him. At the least he had brought him to the service areas, regularly, up in the offices where he could look down on the punters." He shrugged again. "They're both dead. There are going to be some questions we'll never be able to answer."

She nodded, pushed her chair back, sipped at the second cup of coffee. "How's Joshua, Carol?"

The mention of his family made Charlie smile. "Yeah, not bad. Joshua actually slept for a good while last night. Carol is still struggling, but you know, she'll be okay. We'll make it."

"You should take a couple of hours off. Spend some time with her before the next job." A shadow crossed his face, he glanced down at the napkin in his hand. "I will, I was going to put in for some leave to be honest."

"Good idea. Oh yeah and I got you this." She held out a spotty plastic bag. "Well not you, Joshua."

"Tanya, you shouldn't have. Bloody hell, this stuff's not cheap. Carol's going to be chuffed but really, you didn't have to do that."

"Nah, well I was on the site and I saw them – cute little suits. I don't know if it'll fit, don't know much about babies but you can always send it back." She was blushing.

He walked over and bent down, gave her a quick peck on the cheek. It was hard to tell but she thought he might have been blushing as well. "You'll have to come round one weekend, meet the family, see him in his new clothes." He had opened the bag now, pulled out the top and pants and was holding them up in front of him, grinning.

"It's been okay hasn't it, Charlie? I mean you were very good, you must have been a bit brassed off, me coming in on the case, but it was okay wasn't it?"

He nodded, "Yeah. It was fine. Main thing is we cracked it, and we saved Jane. I need to tell you though," he paused, swallowed. "I'm putting in for a transfer."

"Oh, why?"

"Well, I think it might be best if I go somewhere else, start afresh. Carol's up for a move, I reckon it'll be good for her. I've enjoyed working with you Tanya, I wouldn't mind doing it again sometime, but well, I need to go somewhere new."

She nodded and turned away, touched a finger to the corner of her eye. They could have been friends, she was sure of it. Oh well, she was better on her own. Less stress, fewer disappointments.

* * *

When at last she arrived home, the house was in darkness, but it was warm, and the cleaner had been – all was tidy and neat. It was like a picture in a home decorating magazine. The only sound was the click as the smart thermostat detected her presence and turned up the heat.

There was a parcel on the table, the spotty design told her what had arrived without the need to open it. Anyway, she slit along the top with her scissors and pulled out the little blue suit. It was cute, a kitten and a puppy appliquéd onto the short-sleeved top, bigger than the last thing she'd bought for Charlie's son, something intended for Joshua to grow into. She didn't remove it from the plastic bag. The returns label was inside, and the thing was quickly

225

prepared for sending back. This would mean a credit on her account. She needed new jeans to replace the ones ruined on the scaffolding. With a glass of wine on the desk beside her, Tanya logged on and scrolled through the images. Maybe she'd get herself a new handbag as well, a scarf, stuff for herself. There was plenty of room yet in her new dressing room.

The End

List of characters

The Team:

Charlie Lambert – Detective Inspector

Charlie is tall and good looking. He is married to Carol who is suffering from post-natal depression. He is looking for his first high profile case as he climbs the professional ladder.

Robert (Bob) Scunthorpe – Detective Chief Inspector

A decent and honourable senior officer who supports the officers under his control but is realistic about what is required of them to do the job and bring him results.

Tanya Miller – Detective Inspector

Early thirties. Slim and fit, vain, selfish and ambitious, always striving to prove herself. A shopaholic, she has recently returned to Oxford where she had been working in the missing persons section.

Sue Rollinson – Detective Constable

Young, keen, hard worker. Unmarried, from a largish family, father dead, mother an estate agent.

Paul Harris – Detective Sergeant

A plodder. Recently married and a bit of a bloke. Doesn't really get the whole political correctness issue. Lives in a rental flat with his wife Nicole.

Kate Lewis – Detective Constable

Fifty, heading for retirement. Content with her life and achievements but refuses to be side lined due to her age and lack of professional progression.

Dan Price – Detective Constable

Young and insecure. Quiet and keeps his head down. Lives at home with his parents and one kid sister who is still at school.

Simon Hewitt – medical examiner

Tall, handsome, kind and sympathetic.

Moira – mortuary receptionist

Abrupt and unfriendly but tolerated by outsiders and affectionately so by the mortuary staff as she runs the place so efficiently.

Tony Stanley – retired inspector who mentored Tanya.

The public:

Sarah Dickinson

23, 5'4", long blond hair, blue eyes. Book shop manageress.

Steve Blakely

26, blogger, financial advisor. 5'8", a bit of a ponce. Brown hair, hazel eyes. Sarah's boyfriend.

George Simpson

Manager of the motorway services, fussy, fat, middle aged, sweaty and officious.

Peter Harper

Occasional odd job man for Simpson, self-employed, gardener and house clearer.

Millie Roberts

Twenty years old. Slender, 5'6", blond and pretty; we meet her with her friend Sonja. She has one brother, Carl.

Jane Mackie

Snarky and bad tempered, a young teen who can't believe the shit she has to put up with.

If you enjoyed this book, please let others know by leaving a quick review on Amazon. Also, if you spot anything untoward in the paperback, get in touch. We strive for the best quality and appreciate reader feedback.

editor@thebookfolks.com

www.thebookfolks.com

Other books by Diane Dickson:

TWIST OF TRUTH
TANGLED TRUTH
BONE BABY
LEAVING GEORGE
WHO FOLLOWS
THE GRAVE
PICTURES OF YOU
LAYERS OF LIES
DEPTHS OF DECEPTION
YOU'RE DEAD
SINGLE TO EDINBURGH

Made in the USA
San Bernardino, CA
01 July 2018